Stories From The Well

Splashes of Living Water
in the Desert of Life

By Kim Zweygardt

Illustrated by Kary Zweygardt
Photos by Diane Shay

Published by
Accipter Media,
Accipiter Consulting Group, Inc.
PO Box 1234
Guthrie, OK 73044, U.S.A.
http://www.AccipiterMedia.com

All rights reserved. No part of this book may be reproduced in any form without written permission from Accipiter Media.
Copyright © 2007, Kim Zweygardt

First Edition
ISBN 978-0-9787615-3-0

All references are from the New International Version (NIV) Bible, unless otherwise noted.
The NIV Study Bible, Copyright © 1985 by The Zondervan Corporation

Dedication and Acknowledgments

To Jesus for without You my story would be meaningless to write. Thank You for all You have done in my life and all You are going to do! I am grateful for Your grace.

Thank you to my family, especially my husband Kary, and my daughter, Lauren. You have endured months of preoccupation, fending for yourself with meals and laundry and I am ever grateful to you both for putting up with me. Many nights the only way you knew I was still alive was the crack of light under my office door! Jordan & Britt, you're lucky you missed most of it, but thank you all for believing I could do this. Bar none, I have the greatest family in the world...and a bag of chips! And Kary, 'SMOOGLY!'

Thank you to those who shared their stories. If I didn't get it right, it is totally my fault because you all eloquently shared your hearts: Sharon & Kim Leeper, Judy Epp, Kacy Griffin, Kristi Powell, Trisha Harkness, Vonnie Oaks, Julie Gallentine and Pastor Scott Miller. Without you, there would be no stories. May God bless each of you richly!

I wish I could name everyone who has influenced my life in Christ, but there is not room so I only mention the following: Pastors Kent & Joyce Morgan, Atwood, KS, Pastors Joe & Cheryl Briseno, Effingham, IL, Pastors Rich & Ingrid Garcia, Lovelock, NV, and Pastors David & Jackie Butler of St. Francis Community Church, St. Francis, KS. In the words of Pastor David, "Ya'll ROCK!"

Thank you to my "real family," Mom, Daddy, Sharon & Shelly, as well as my SFCC family for your love & support and to the Apostolic Regional Prayer Council, past & present: Julie, Lonnie, Sharon, Edna and Orvella for the many ways you love & bless me!

Finally, thank you to Roy Jones of Accipiter Media for his work on this book! God still works though Divine Appointments!

To God be the Glory!

Kim Zweygardt

Preface

Beloved,

I don't know why this book is in your hands, but God does. I don't know what you need in your life, but God does. I don't know how God does miracles and changes lives, but I know He does.

How can I be so sure? He has done it for me and the other men and women whose stories are included in this book.

I met Jesus at a Lay Witness meeting when I was 15. But for whatever reason, I couldn't take in all that He offered me then. It was 20 years and much heartache later that He offered me a way out of the depths of my sin and offered me His Life. That was over 15 years ago and I've never looked back.

I wrote this book based on the story in John 4:1-42 where many years ago a sinful woman met Jesus at a well in Samaria.

Let's go back to that well and meet the woman there, but let's also meet other men and women who have been to the well. Even more importantly, let's go meet Jesus there. He is waiting.

God bless you as you go.

Kim Zweygardt
January 7, 2007

Contents

Preface iii

1 The Divine Appointment 1

2 The Divine Encounter 5

3 "Give Me A Drink" 13

4 Journey to the Well 19

5 Ordinary Day, Extraordinary Jesus 23

6 "It Doesn't Matter How You Got Here" 31

7 Religion Can't Bring Life 43

8 Truth = Freedom 49

9 Natural Need, Supernatural Answer 57

10 An Unlikely Source 65

11 Leaving the Old Behind 75

12 Walking a New Path 83

13 Streams of Living Water 91

My Prayer for You 97

"Those who knew the word of God couldn't see the Word of God."

One

THE DIVINE APPOINTMENT

He was as weary as he had ever been.

He leaned forward into the hint of a breeze looking older than his years, his footsteps heavy from heat and exhaustion, his sandals making little imprint in the desolate road.

Centuries of travelers had walked this road, but their thousands of footsteps had not polished or paved the rocky surface. The occasional gust swirled the sand from the crevices, obscuring the slight imprint of his friend's sandals, obliterating any evidence they'd passed this way.

He looked back. Already the timeless sands had shifted and his footprints were gone. He could have been anyone or no one traveling through Samaria.

A bead of sweat dripped from his brow, slid down the side of his long nose and into his curling, dark beard. He ignored it, brow furrowed in concentration, keeping his footing on the rocky road.

The hills undulated in an endless panorama of green and tan, broken only by the rocky outcroppings and silver leafed olive trees. He climbed a small rise and stopped to catch his breath.

He was tired to the bone.

He blew his breath upward in a attempt to cool his face and looked up.

"How long, Father?"

With the heavy sleeve of his coarse tunic, he mopped his brow and waited, cocking his head to listen and smiled, remembering a different journey and Joseph's kind face.

"Are we there yet, Abba?"

"No, son. Not yet."

Today's question was deeper.

He shook his foot to dislodge the rock that had worked its way into his sandal. Even his leathery feet, so used to standing in the carpenter's shop and walking the rough roads from village to village, were suffering on this journey. He had worn a blister on his big toe and it hurt.

He squinted up into the hot sun and asked again, "Father?"

The question wasn't about anything in particular, just that simple asking, listening for the softest whisper of His voice. But Abba was silent.

For the most part, so were his friends. The men straggled along the road ahead of him, not noticing he'd lagged behind. A long day had been made longer by the journey from Judea.

He had not been ready to leave Judea with so many coming to the water to be baptized, but the argument between John's disciples and the Jews drew attention to him.

It wasn't yet his time.

Those who knew the words of God couldn't see The Word of God. All they could see was that it wasn't their way.

And for all their laws, none brought Life.

Since first light they'd traveled toward Galilee. Not stopping as the sun rose hot above them. The shortest route made longer by their weariness.

He closed his eyes for a moment remembering the cool deep waters of the Jordan.

The steady stream of humanity stepping into the water, eager for renewal.

Rough fishermen and shepherds, tears cleansing dusty faces as they stepped into cool green waters.

Fathers embracing sons.

Sisters and brothers on the bank, excitedly hopping from one foot to the other.

Mothers with babes in arms, tears streaming down patient faces, waiting their turn.

The religious leaders in their proper dress, phylacteries flowing, standing a long way off. Uninvolved, but coolly observing it all.

Salty tears washed away in the clean water.

Sin revealed. Repentance unveiled. New life found. Though most of them who came probably couldn't articulate that was what they had come for.

How close they were and couldn't see it! But it was not time.

"When, Father, when?"

Again, the heavens were silent.

Oh, to throw off the humanity that clothed him!

Suddenly, the softest whisper.

He stood still, listening. It was not the sound of the dry grass rustling on the hillside nor the wind in the olive trees or the faint rumble of the voices of the men he loved straggling along on the hilly, dusty road.

"But they say to worship here on Mt. Gerazim and we say..." John's voice drifted on the breeze in the endless argument over the most holy site to worship.

The whisper brushed his ear again bringing a flood of compassion. He closed his eyes, the grittiness of the day washed away as the picture in his heart brought a lump to his throat.

His stomach grumbled to be fed. His feet still hurt. He was dry-as-a-bone thirsty. His humanity cried out for attention, but the divine called him for another purpose.

The path turned sharply and with a shout, Peter ran toward the well. The small grove of trees and scrubby bushes that shaded the deep well dug by Jacob many years before brought welcome relief from the heat. Glimmering down below, a tiny village nestled against the southeastern slope of Mt. Ebal. An obscure place.

Except for the Father.

"Master! Rabboni, you look weary. Sit here and we will go into the town and find food and a place to stay."

He smiled, nodding his agreement.

They would surely meet her on the road.

Would they notice?

Heaven stirred answering his anticipation.

Did she know that today her life would change and she would never be the same?

His friends disappeared around the bend. She could not be far off. His smile never wavered, lighting his dark eyes from within as he sat down to wait.

"There was no hope for her. Wasn't that what they said?"

Two

THE DIVINE ENCOUNTER

She stood shifting from one foot to the next just inside the door of her small house, half wanting to slip out unnoticed, the other half wanting to make a scene.

It was already midday and too hot to go for water. Surely, the neighbors had heard the early morning argument that began with Darius grumbling about the house and ended with a litany of her failures. And of course the accusations and reminders of the past.

There had been a time she would have slammed the door and left once and for all, letting everyone within earshot know she didn't care what they thought of her.

Those days were long gone.

Still, she pulled the door shut sharply as she stepped out into the bright day and smiled thinly as it made a satisfying thump. It would do.

The empty water jar that had begun the rift sat by the door. She lifted it to her shoulder, stepping out of the small courtyard and into the narrow street.

Darius was no where to be seen. Probably drinking with the same friends who had regaled him with stories of her past. As if he didn't know, but hearing it from another man was something different, she supposed.

She didn't know why they wouldn't leave her alone. She knew she was no longer beautiful, but Darius found her intriguing. He said it was the way she tossed her head and swayed her hips when she walked to the market.

She blushed, remembering.

Now she looked so common. The earthenware jar was rough, her gown woven of plain brown cloth, her face and hands darkened from hard work. Darius had stuck by her for five years, but the years had not been good to her.

One thing for sure, her life had not turned out the way she thought it would.

The narrow street twisted and turned through the village. She knew every stone and small house that sat tumbling along the mountainside, higgledy-piggledy, almost on top of each other as they crowded the narrow road. The small village was drab and common and she hated it, preferring to think of the more exotic places she'd heard about from the merchants who traveled this road.

She tuned out the sounds of life in Sychar, walking alone down the narrow street of the village as if she preferred it that way, eyes straight ahead, full lips frozen into a thin smile that never reached her eyes. She'd darkened them with kohl in a vain attempt to hide the swollen lids from prying eyes, but she knew, just as she heard the neighbors business, they'd heard the morning's argument with Darius.

The street of merchants was alive with laughter and conversation. The woman instinctively straightened her shoulders, pasting her smile even more firmly on her face, her ears attuned to the conversation they never tired of and sauntered past them. Conversation sputtered and she heard her name. Tossing her head, she turned away. If they wanted to talk, let them talk.

The path turned sharply as well-worn street gave way to the steep and rocky path to the well. She could no longer see them, but their voices carried on the languid air.

Darius had stormed out that morning before breakfast. They hadn't eaten the bread she'd baked and her stomach rumbled its protest. She'd been too sick at heart to eat and now she felt woozy. She sagged under the weight of the jar, suddenly exhausted from the I-don't-care game she'd played with the village women.

The tears came easily. It was the usual argument. She'd change the past if she could, but she couldn't. When he threatened to throw her out, she'd screamed back, "I don't care!" but he knew she did. She had no place else to go.

A burst of laughter rippled on the breeze. They were probably still talking about her. Most of the time she could pretend she didn't care what they said, but today, pretending didn't work.

She swallowed the bitterness as bile rose in her throat and turned toward the well. No matter how she felt, they needed water.

Darius had been angry as it was. If he came home and no water...

His voice joined the Voices in her head.

"How stupid *are* you? Can't you do anything right? I don't blame them for throwing you out and I might do it myself if you don't change!"

"Look at her! Doesn't have sense enough to go for water before the heat of the day?"

"She's so stuck up! Doesn't want to associate with us, I guess."

"And with her reputation? Who does she think she is?"

She knew well enough what they said about her. She'd said it often enough herself.

Her dark wavy hair lay heavy on her neck as the sweat trickled down between her shoulder blades under the heavy shawl. She longed to take it off and let the breeze blow her hair. She was out of sight of the women, what would it matter?

She argued with herself.

"Leave it on. What if someone saw you and told Darius?"

"Who?"

"Doesn't matter. You know what they'd say. 'Loose!' 'Immoral!' A married woman can't be seen without a proper head covering."

"You're not married."

It always came down to that.

She was not like the others.

Never had been.

Never would be.

A sudden breeze swirled stinging gravel into a whirling dust devil, filling her eyes with grit as it tangled her dress around her legs. She angrily pulled at her dress. She would not cry any more.

She had cried enough for one day.

She'd cried enough for a lifetime.

Her face was still puffy from the morning's tears, her arms bearing the bruises of Darius' grasp.

Why did she try to defend herself?

He would believe what he wanted. He would believe what they said. He just wouldn't believe her.

"Why should he?" The accusing Voice returned.

Without meaning to, she cried out loud, "but I haven't done anything!" Her voice echoed across the green valley.

And yet she had.

Time and time again.

Bad choices.

Wrong choices.

Sinful and scandalous choices.

Her sins were unforgivable. She'd been told that often enough.

"If only..." She shook her head at the useless thought, but the Voice took up the refrain.

"If only, what? You could start over? If only Jonah meant it when he said he'd marry you? If only the elders hadn't found you together?"

She'd been such a fool! Why would the son of a rich man want to marry a girl from a poor family? But her heart had leapt at every glance and she'd been glad every time he spoke to her. He had said she was beautiful.

Her eyes softened at the memory.

"Fool! Fool!"

The Voice was back.

It was true. She was a fool and Mama and Papa had never forgiven her.

Neither had the village.

And neither had Thomas.

She'd cried for days when Papa arranged their marriage, but his face was like flint.

"Papa! He's so old! And I heard his wife died just to get away from him! No, Papa! Please, I beg you!"

Mama cried too, but Papa said it was from her broken heart. They had no choice, he said. No one else wanted her.

Thomas was much, much older, but in need of a wife, though he refused to pay the bride price. He was cocky and cunning and the scar running from his lip to his ear gave him a cruel look which matched his reputation. It was well earned.

She could never please him.

Ever.

He laughed at her as she ran from him. His appetites were those of a man half his age. Her wrists still bore the scars from him "teaching her a lesson." It pleased him that she had no place to go. Not that it stopped him from throwing her out.

She could still smell his hot breath and see his leering eyes as he threw the certificate of divorce at her where she'd fallen in the street.

"Now, see what your stubbornness has gotten you! You don't know when you've got it good!"

She adjusted the water jar as the path climbed the mountain. The loose gravel was treacherous on the steep path. She'd fallen once and there was hell to pay when she got home with no water and a broken jar, not to mention the skinned knees and bruises that kept her from moving as quickly as Thomas wanted.

She'd been relieved when he kicked her out, thinking Mama would let her come home, but Papa's bitterness was too deep. Mama answered the door, but Papa pushed her back inside, saying they no longer had a daughter.

She never went home again.

She was young, then, with fiery eyes and pretty dark hair. And there were always men who needed a woman around the house.

She grasped an olive branch to steady herself as memories came unbidden of all the men and mistakes she'd made. Suddenly, the jar was too heavy to carry and she could not take another step under the weight of the jar and the weight of her life.

Her legs felt like trees.

It was just too hard.

There was no hope for her. Wasn't that what they said?

She'd sat so quietly in the Court of Women at the Temple when the Rabbi taught about the God of compassion.

The God that was sending the Messiah, the Restorer, to save them.

It didn't even matter that no one sat with her.

In her heart burned a flicker of hope. She finally gathered courage enough to ask one of the women if the Messiah was coming for everyone.

"Not for you, dear. He's coming for those who are good." The woman's eyes were cold.

Her faced flushed remembering the mocking laughter as the woman repeated her question to the others.

"She thought the Messiah was for her! Oh, that's a good one!"

"What is she doing here anyway?"

She knew she didn't belong and never went back.

The memories faded as she heard voices around the bend. The little band of men stepped aside to let her pass on the narrow road.

They seemed kind enough, but she lowered her eyes and did not speak. She'd heard stories about the Jews.

"If they knew you they wouldn't be so kind!"

The mocking Voice never left her. At the slightest provocation it was there reminding her of the past, as if the men and women of Sychar needed help!

She sighed with relief as she climbed the rise. The well was up ahead. She'd draw her water, rest a moment in the shade and figure out a way to make Darius trust her. She couldn't go through it again. She didn't have the strength. She was as weary as she had ever been.

"One thing for sure, her life had not turned out the way she thought it would."

"He had come here just for this."

Three

"GIVE ME A DRINK"

He waited, listening to his Father, watching her quietly from a distance.

The earthen water jar almost overshadowed her. She was not pretty exactly, but there was something about her that was attractive, even struggling under the weight of the jar. It was still empty, but with her heavy footsteps, it might have weighed 3,000 shekels.

Her dark eyes were puffy though she'd tried to disguise the splotchy skin that bore witness to the morning's argument. The sun had baked her tears into trails of pale salt from her cheeks to her chin. Her attempts to wipe them away had only smeared her face with the blowing sands of Samaria. All of it spoke to him of her heartache.

His heart swelled with compassion.

She looked older than her years and was poorly dressed. She must have been pretty at one time, but now she looked harassed and hopeless. Everything about her testified that life had not been kind.

The compassion had not left him from the moment the Father had whispered her name in his ear. He longed to gather her like a lamb into his arms to comfort her, but he knew she would not understand.

She looked so lonely. The heavy cloak hid the scars of life from prying eyes, but her scars were not hidden from him.

Seeing through his Father's eyes, looking past the brokenness, he could see clearly what her life was meant to be.

Could joy and sorrow share the same tears?

She was His Beloved!

He had come here just for this. He had come for her and all the others broken by the cares of life. It was not fully his time, but it was *her* time! Heaven and all of heaven's angels waited in hushed anticipation.

This moment had been set in eternity.

This woman.

This day.

Freed from the Kingdom of Darkness! Enthroned as a Princess in His Light!

Bondage broken!

He could almost hear the links of heavy chain snap, the demons groaning in disappointment. She could choose freedom, and yet she'd chosen bondage over and over. He could only offer it to her. The choice was hers.

"Give me a drink."

The woman stood up quickly, startled by his voice and almost let go of the rope holding her jar. The deep voice was kind, but she hadn't seen him sitting there.

She peered into the shadows, taking in his robe and sandals, the dark skin and beard. She looked again and saw the prayer shawl.

A Jew! Why wasn't he with the others?

She stepped away from the well, turning her back on him as she tossed her head and asked, "Why would you, a Jew, ask a Samaritan woman for a drink?" Her words were bricks, building a wall to keep him out.

He spoke again, gently, but firmly.

"If you knew the gift of God and who asked you for a drink, you would have asked him and he would have given you living water!"

He looked so common, yet he spoke with authority. He stepped toward her, as she turned towards his words. His dark, compassionate eyes caught hers and did not waver.

He looked at her as if he knew her. But not like other men. Plenty of men had looked at her before, but this was different. He looked at her as if he knew everything about her and yet he did not seem to judge her. His eyes held only empathy.

Who was this man offering her "living water"?

And who'd even heard of such a thing from this well? *Living water.* Suddenly, her mouth was so dry, she could barely talk. She had never been thirstier.

He watched the naked longing transform the worn-out features of her face.

"But sir, where would you get this living water, for the well is deep and you have nothing to draw with?"

Her tongue was thick from desire as her thoughts tumbled over each other awaiting his reply.

"Who was this man? A prophet? An angel? Perhaps a vision brought on by the heat and my tears and longing?"

Something drew her to him. She could see her whole life reflected in the deep stillness of his eyes, but healed and whole somehow. Her life, but a different life. Her face, but not the one she saw in the glass darkly.

His voice broke her reverie.

"He who drinks of this water will thirst again," he said. "But he who drinks of the water I give will never thirst again! Indeed, the water I give will become a well of water springing up within to give eternal life!"

She had been told many, many times that there was no hope of eternal life for her and yet here was this stranger saying she should just ask him and he would give her eternal life?

"Sir," she cried, falling to her knees. "Give me this water that I might not thirst again and have to keep coming here to the well to draw!"

Long dead hope flickered to life and burned within her bosom.

And then he said, "Go and get your husband and come back."

She reeled as if taking a punch she hadn't seen coming. She gasped for breath, but the world was devoid of air.

She should have known.

What the stranger offered wasn't for her.

She fought for composure, trying in vain to paste the I-don't-care smile back on her face, but it wouldn't stay in place.

She turned her head so he wouldn't see her watery eyes. She wanted to lie! She had lived with Darius for five years as if his wife, how would this stranger ever know?

He watched her quietly, the warmth in his eyes never wavering as she stood to her feet, her olive skin flushing in shame as she thought, "He doesn't know who I am. And even if I lie to him, I'll always know the truth."

She sighed heavily as her new life disappeared like a vapor.

"I have no husband."

She breathed the words so softly any other man would have strained to hear.

All creation had waited breathlessly for her answer. And at that moment the Truth echoed into eternity.

He had seen hope, then defeat play across her features and wanted to weep. She didn't know that her redemption was nigh!

"You speak the truth when you say you have no husband, for you have had five husbands and even now the man you live with is not your husband."

He spoke quietly affirming the truth, his voice echoing the love of the Father.

Snap! The sound of chains broken!

Her head covering fell back exposing her face and hair, but she didn't notice. She stood before the stranger with nothing hidden.

Years of shame transformed by Truth!

He had said, "You tell the truth" and with that Truth, she was healed and made whole somehow! Truth had freed her when hope ignited her soul.

"Sir," she said, "I know the Messiah is coming. And when he comes he will explain everything to us."

"I am He," Jesus said. "The One speaking to you"

Her eyes were opened with his words. This man *was* the Messiah! He was the Messiah and he loved her!

Her face lit up and she looked like a young girl again. Without thinking, she ran to where he stood, standing on her tiptoes to kiss him on both cheeks and then she was gone!

His laughter followed her as she left her jar behind, running pell mell down the hill toward the village, almost knocking Peter flat as the disciples came around the bend. They looked astonished, but she did not even murmur an "I'm sorry". She had to get to Sychar and tell everyone she knew that she had met the Messiah!

"He told me everything I've ever done!"

Soon a large crowd made their way to the well to meet Jesus because of what the woman had told them.

There were those who refused to come saying, "She has gone crazy."

And some laughed that a woman like her would have met the Messiah. But many did come and listen to his words and believed that the Messiah had truly come to Sychar.

He stayed with the Samaritans for two more days. Many had believed after hearing the woman's testimony, "He told me everything I've ever done." But after he taught them, many more believed saying to the woman, "We no longer believe because of what you said, for we have heard for ourselves and know that this Jesus is really the Savior of the world."

"Beloved, are you thirsty?"

Four

JOURNEY TO THE WELL

Beloved, did your heart beat with anticipation as you read the story, knowing what was to come?

Was it so familiar that you couldn't wait for this poor, desperate woman to meet Jesus so she could find what you have found?

Do you remember your first gulp of Living Water? How hot and thirsty you were when you met the Savior and you can't wait for others to meet him too!

Even today, thirst is a distant memory because everyday He pours out Living Water and you drink your fill!

Or did you pick up this book on a whim? You don't know much about Bible stories and that whole "Living Water thing" doesn't make much sense, but now you're a little curious.

Could it be true? Is it all about meeting Jesus or is there more? Surely it can't be that easy?

Maybe tears stung your eyes as the woman trudged that steep path with her only companions the accusing Voices of the past and present, telling her the future will be just more and more of the same.

You know just how she feels because those accusing Voices accompany you, too.

You've made mistakes. And in your heart of hearts you wonder if maybe those mistakes are too big for even God to forgive. You sure don't want to tell anyone about them, so you cover it up with a pasted-on smile, but inside your heart is breaking.

And the weight of life just gets heavier and heavier.

You're on a long, hot dusty road and you don't even know where it leads. You'd like to get off the nowhere path, but you think you missed the last exit.

This road is all you can remember and all you know, so you just keep on, keeping on, ignoring your parched throat, doing your best, but still coming up short, somehow.

One thing for sure; life isn't what you thought it would be.

Beloved, are you thirsty?

Are you so weary that if you sat down to rest, you aren't sure you'd ever get back up?

Maybe you've met Christ, but somehow, all that abundant life seems like it's for someone else and not for you.

You've made too many mistakes.

You don't seem to be able to stop old patterns and habits.

You believe, but so much of this Christian life feels like just going through the motions.

You do all the right stuff, all the church stuff but it doesn't change the deep, longing in your heart. You feel a little better on Sunday, but by Tuesday, the thirst is even worse.

"Sir! Where do I get this Living Water that I might not thirst again?"

It is the heart cry of every man, woman and child and it can only be answered by doing as the woman did: *crying out to the Savior*.

I am the Woman at the Well. Her story is my story. I tried everything I knew to quench the terrible thirst within my soul and nothing changed until I met Jesus.

This book is a journey to the well.

Here you will find Stories about those who have gone to the well before you.

It is a journey not just to the well, but to a place where Christ is waiting for us.

It is a journey where we come empty and leave overflowing.

It is a journey to a transformed life, an abundant life, a life where the River of Life flows, filling the well to overflowing, to a place where once you've been there, nothing else will satisfy.

Come with me, Beloved!
He is waiting!

"...miracles happen every day, but...we don't see them because we aren't looking."

Five

ORDINARY DAY—
EXTRAORDINARY JESUS

July 3, 2004 began much like every other summer day on a Kansas cattle ranch. My sister Sharon and her husband, Kim Leeper were up early and outside in the cool of the morning to tend to chores, but as the day wore on it got hot! Still there was plenty of hard work to keep a man busy. Especially a man like Kim, who is driven to do a job right.

Kim is one of those rare individuals that everyone likes. Not a big man, but a man with a big heart, he is everyone's favorite uncle. His teasing nature often got him in hot water in younger years, but his integrity and love of people made him a good husband, father and friend.

At 51, he had not slowed down. His passion was life on the ranch and improving the line of cattle they bred at Mule Creek Ranch.

His wife, Sharon, was another of those people that just naturally draws people to her. Kim never had trouble finding extra help during busy times on the ranch because Sharon kept the cowboys well fed. Smart, blonde and pretty, she was well-known for her cherry pies among the cowboys who came to help during the busy times at Mule Creek and the hunters that filled the Bunk House during hunting season. A former rodeo queen, twirler, and Valedictorian of the Class of '72, she'd opted to marry her high school sweetheart instead of pursue college and career and life with Kim was always an adventure! His grin still made her melt after 32 years. They loved life on the ranch and were good partners. Life was good.

That day they'd worked hard, but when the work was done, it was time to relax. Kim played just as hard as he worked and loved to have a good time. That beautiful summer was perfect for a ride on his new motorcycle.

Kim had enjoyed motorcycles all of his life and with their kids grown and mostly on their own, he'd bought the bike he'd always dreamed of.

Kim and Sharon live the western life of cowboying on horseback, so it had been a kick the summer before when they had ridden from their ranch up through the Black Hills of South Dakota including the site of the World's Biggest Motorcycle Rally in Sturgis, South Dakota!

That Saturday afternoon was a shorter trip, just into a nearby town and back home before dark.

Mule Creek Ranch lies in Comanche County, Kansas in the scenic Gyp hills. Scenic highway 160 is a narrow, hilly, two-lane black top with steep ditches on either side that connects Coldwater and Medicine Lodge as it cuts through the historic hills. It is an area of red dirt bluffs and plateaus where Indian warriors once rode through the deep canyons and along the bluffs of the creek hunting buffalo. There is still abundant wild-life in this beautiful place, well known for the mule deer that feed along the creek that bears their name.

Kim and Sharon ran into friends in Medicine Lodge who wanted them to stay for supper, but they'd begged off in order to get home before the deer come out to feed in the pastures along Mule Creek.

There is a special time of summer in Kansas when the heat of the day gives way to the cool of the evening and the shadows of clouds turn the distant hills to purple and the fields to gold as if lit from within.

They rode through the still evening, as Sharon says, "Not speeding, just toodling along" when disaster struck just three miles from home.

As they topped a small hill, a large doe was quietly feeding in the south ditch. Kim nodded at Sharon that he'd seen it, but the sudden appearance of the motorcycle spooked her. Instead of leaping the fence to disappear into the brush alongside the highway, it ran the opposite way crossing the narrow highway right in front of them!

There was no way to avoid a collision.

Kim laid the bike down, skidding into the startled deer. The motorcycle was no match for the doe and the impact threw Kim over the handlebars of the bike, hitting the pavement hard on his right shoulder and head, smacking his brain against the left side of his skull causing what his neurologist called a "non-survivable" head injury. Kim landed face down at the edge of the highway as the motorcycle ground to a stop in the middle of the road.

Kim has few memories of the moment of impact, but Sharon vividly remembers skidding down the highway expecting every bone in her body would be broken. Instead, the rough pavement shredded her heavy riding clothes, burning through her pants and boots to raw flesh. When she got up, the diamond of her wedding ring had been sheared off and the flesh of her hand burned away leaving a tendon in her thumb exposed and second and third degree burns on her hands, arms, chest and legs. Shakily, she tried to run back down the highway where Kim laid screaming and gasping for breath, already incoherent from brain swelling.

Their cell phone was at home, but it wouldn't have mattered. The area is desolate with no cell towers, few houses and little traffic.

That evening, there was no traffic as Sharon paced and cried, frantic with shock and pain, doing her best to comfort Kim, and praying desperately for someone to come along. For two hours, she sat with her husband at the edge of the highway, screaming and crying out to God, not sure what to do.

Darkness was falling and finally, there was no choice but to try to go for help. Sharon could barely walk as the hours had stiffened her muscles and heightened the searing pain from the weeping burns. The nearest neighbor was two miles away, but there was no choice. If Kim didn't get help soon he would die.

The accident occurred in a small valley between two hills and as she hobbled to the top of the hill toward the nearest neighbor, she looked back at her husband lying at the edge of the road. From the distance he looked small, but she did not have the strength to move him. The motorcycle still lay in the highway where it had come to rest. If someone finally came along and she was not there to flag them down, there would be another accident and Kim might be run over in the dark.

Stiffly, she turned and made her way slowly back down the hill to sit beside him. She would not leave him. They had been together for almost 32 years of marriage, but their life together had begun long before that.

Sharon and Kim were not just high school sweethearts, but junior high school sweethearts.

The Leeper family lived a block away from the our house in Protection, Kansas. Kim was a blonde and freckled 8th grader when he first noticed the girl with the long blonde hair and sparkling blue eyes that lived down the street. In a town of 800, you made your own fun. It was one giant neighborhood so all the kids in town gathered for shooting hoops or games of kick-the-can on summer nights. Our backyard and driveway basketball hoop was often the center of activity and Kim began to show up more and more often.

He was known for a characteristic loud whistle and that became the signal for Sharon to step out to the back fence when he would just happen to walk down the alley between the houses. There had never been anyone else for either of them since those days of first love.

When his friends or family couldn't find him at his house, he was usually at ours. They had married young and worked together building a life and raising their three kids. They had spent very little time apart in those years and Sharon would not leave him now.

She had been praying desperately since the accident, "Lord, Kim is a godly man and he loves you! Please, You cannot let him die out here like this!" She was past desperation as she made her way back to him crying out to God once more, "God, You have to send someone to help us!"

Suddenly, headlights pierced the darkness. A man traveling that lonely road with a satellite phone came over the hill and called 9-1-1 for her. Help was on the way.

I am a Certified Registered Nurse Anesthetist (CRNA). I put people to sleep for surgery, but I am also called to help with trauma in the emergency room. I hear it over and over again.

"It happened so fast!

"We didn't have time to react!"

"Our lives changed in an instant!"

I think we would all agree, either from things that have happened to us or to people we know, that life is fragile. We go through our days thinking we have some control over things, but it is only when disaster strikes that we ask ourselves, "Who's really in charge of this?"

My sister's story has a happy ending. The ambulance got there. Life-flight flew them to a major trauma hospital. It was the neurosurgeon there who looked at the initial CT scan and said, "This is not a survivable injury."

But God hadn't told that to the hundreds of people who had been mobilized to pray.

The next prediction by the doctors was that if he survived, it would take years of rehabilitation.

It took weeks.

Sharon and Kim celebrated their 32nd wedding anniversary in the hospital, but he was alive and they were together.

I could write this whole book about all the miracles that took place in this circumstance, but that is not what this book is about. Suffice it to say, an ordinary day turned extraordinary when God showed up.

My sister will tell you that there have been changes in their lives that have been hard. My brother-in-law would say the same, but they also know that his life is a miracle. Kim says that miracles happen every day, but most of the time we don't see them because we're not looking for them.

And they both would say that God made a way where there seemed to be no way.

A supernatural God spoke life when in the natural there was only death.

Those many years ago, a lonely, heartbroken woman walked to a well in Samaria. She didn't know it, but she was dying.

For from the moment we are born, our bodies begin the process of dying. Even with modern medicine, death comes eventually.

But death comes in other ways, too.

Life was hard in Samaria.

No modern conveniences.

No medicines to stave off illness.

But the woman was dying from something else.

She had suffered the death of her dreams.

The Bible says, "Hope deferred makes the heart sick." (Proverbs 13:12)

Did her dreams die suddenly or was it slow death and strangulation with every failure?

I would guess she had been like every little girl.

She played and helped her mother in the kitchen and dreamed of the day when she'd have her own home and children. Maybe like many girls, she adored her Papa and wanted to grow up and marry a man just like him!

She had high hopes when she noticed the boys noticing her. And when one boy singled her out for attention? Her heart did back flips!

Was he handsome? Was he kind? Was she sure he was "the one"?

Maybe he flirted with her, but chose another.

We don't know, but we do know that she began a journey that ended at the well with Jesus saying, "You have had five husbands and even now the man you live with is not your husband."

How many times had she gone to the well in Samaria?

It was more than just getting water. It was a social time for women to giggle and gossip together.

Have you ever been part of a group of women? Then you know what I mean.

Did you ever feel left out if they talked about something you knew nothing about?

Can you imagine the feelings of shame and loneliness this woman felt day after day as the women talked about their husbands? Did she try to join in? Did they smirk at her because of her reputation?

She had been married many times. That shows me she'd tried to do the right thing, but in those days, all a man had to do was write out a certificate of divorce and a woman was out on the street.

I am sure her hopes were high each time she went to the altar, but she still ended up alone.

It was a man's world. It didn't take much for a man to move on. Somehow, she'd failed to do what every woman was supposed to do— be a good wife.

Finally, she didn't even bother with the legalities. "It hasn't stopped them from leaving before, so why bother?"

And finally she stopped trying to be one of the girls. They didn't want her, so why try to fit in? She'd go to the well alone.

That day was like so many others.

The trip to the well alone.

The heat of the day and the weight of her life.

It was all so familiar.

Just going through the motions and trying to survive. Forget happiness. She just didn't want to be beat down any further.

But as she walked that familiar, dusty road to the well, she did not know that she was about to encounter the Divine! Jesus knew exactly where she was on that dusty road and God was about to turn her ordinary day into an extraordinary day!

Where are you?

Going through the motions or living a life of adventure?

On the way to the well to get just enough water to survive another day or have you jumped into the River of Living Water?

STORIES FROM THE WELL

Have you been beaten down and your dreams turned to ashes? Was life pretty good, but in one terrible instant, everything changed? The doctor called and the biopsy was cancer? The police are on the phone and your son has been arrested again? Your boss is apologetic, but the economy stinks since 9/11? Your husband says he doesn't love you anymore and he just wants out?

Everyone else seems to have it all together, but you're looking at your life and it is not what you thought your life would be.

The road is dusty and rocky beneath your feet. Your mouth is so dry your tongue sticks to the roof of it. You want to cry, but you've cried too many tears already. You don't know what else to do so you do what you always do. You walk toward the well with the jar getting heavier by the minute and hope that this time is different.

Dear one, it will be! Today is the day of your salvation and Jesus waits for you!

What seems like an ordinary day is about to become extraordinary, not because of what *you've* done, but because of what *He* has done!

Not because of *where you are*, but because of *where He is!*

As you round the last curve and see the well ahead in the clearing, do you see Him waiting there?

Your redemption is here!

Don't forget! Every day's a miracle when God shows up!

Dear Lord,

Thank You that You are a God of miracles. Thank You that you take the ordinary of our lives—both good and bad—and turn it to the extraordinary! Forgive me for the times there have been miracles but I haven't noticed. Open my eyes to You working in my world. Open my eyes to You working in me. Show up in my life where I need help and hope, Lord. Thank You in advance for what You are going to do to turn my ordinary days extraordinary!

In Jesus' Name,

Amen.

"I had come to the end of myself and God was waiting to pick up the pieces."

Six

"DOESN'T MATTER HOW YOU GOT HERE,
THE IMPORTANT THING IS THAT YOU'RE HERE!"

I am the woman at the well. Her story is much like mine or rather mine is like hers!

Though my two sisters might not agree, I was a normal kid! I am the middle child and all that that implies. (Don't argue with me! Argue with all the people who write the birth order books!)

My parents married young as was the custom in the 1950's. Betty Jane Kimberly married Martin Luther Webster, Jr. when Mom was 17 and Daddy, 19, in June, 1953. Soon the Webster house was filled with little girls! Sharon Kay was born a year later, followed by Kimberly Sue in two years and Shelly Rene' followed in two and a half years.

Daddy farmed and worked hard. Mom stayed at home. We went to Sunday School at the Methodist church down the street from our house. We had a nice home, one car, and enough clothes, food and money. We were a typical family of the 1950's. Daddy even survived our teen years with three girls in a one bathroom house sharing one small mirror!

But though we had many good times, things weren't always ideal.

In 1978, Mom and Daddy divorced after years of ups and downs. They married so young, I think they were growing up even as they were raising us. I remember Mom and Daddy arguing many times, but more than that, I remember happy times as a family. Whatever the trouble between Mom and Daddy, we never doubted their love.

I was a good student and active in school. Student Council President. Co-Editor of Yearbook. Band. Vocal Music. Speech and Drama. I was busy, but not popular according to the criteria of the day, but I had a solid group of friends. Together we dreamed of all that life could be.

It was the 1970's and we were "Woooo-maaan! W-O-M-A-N! I'll say it again!"[1] We sang along with Maria Muldaur and Helen Reddy and the commercials that archived the changes between the women who worried about their hands becoming rough doing dishes and the women who could "bring home the bacon" *and* "fry it up in a pan."[2]

Roe v. Wade was making its way through the Supreme Court. Vietnam had become a quagmire and political hot potato. Women left home for the workplace in droves. They were liberated and could make choices that only years before were taboo. It was a heady time to be coming of age.

Super model Cheryl Tiegs graced the cover of nearly every teen magazine in the 1970's. She was our ideal of teen beauty and we all wanted to be tall and thin with long straight blonde hair! My medium length brown hair and green eyes made me feel plain next to my two blonde-haired, blue eyed sisters who had the look that I didn't. I didn't think I'd frighten anybody in a dark alley, but I didn't look the way I wanted to.

Sharon was also a great student, well-liked and popular so I looked for ways to be noticed apart from the things she did. In my estimation, Sharon never did anything wrong! I noticed that the more radical I became the more attention it garnered and so I became very liberal and even more vocal in my views on *everything!* It is embarrassing now, but at the time, I loved it! I wrote letters to the editor of local and state newspapers on the need for sex education in the schools, much to my parents' chagrin.

I had discovered that there were boys who didn't think I was plain and liked my zany, wild personality. I dated several boys until I began going steady my junior year.

Rebellion was my middle name and I was insistent on marching to the beat of my own drummer even if the drummer was drumming up trouble! It was pretty tame for what was going on in the world in 1973, but my major form of rebellion was missing my curfew and I was grounded almost weekly as my parents fought for control over my hard headed behavior! But given the next chance, I still went my own way! (Sorry, Mom.)

The 70's mantra was sex, drugs, and rock and roll, but in small-town Kansas, you didn't have to go very "far out" to be different.

And I loved being different and the attention it got from boys. My conversations with my girlfriends were peppered with talk of who had kissed who and "how far" they had gone.

In 1975, I quit college and got married for the first time to my high school sweetheart. It was my greatest rebellion as Mom and Daddy begged me to not do it.

We'd been dating for several years and I had seen evidence of his immaturity, controlling nature, and temper, but his temper had never been directed at me...until after the wedding.

Three weeks of wedded bliss turned ugly when I didn't peel the skin off a tomato for a salad! He slapped me so hard, I hit the wall and slid to the floor. By the time I got up from the floor, I was a different person. I had always been fiery and stood my ground, but now I was afraid.

And ashamed.

A few months later, I arrived on my parents door step in the middle of the night, hurt and hysterical.

On the outside, the "old Kim" was back after a few weeks of healing. I filed for divorce and went back to college.

But I was broken on the inside and I was looking for something or someone to fill in the broken places. I was on a mission, looking for love in all the wrong places and always with the wrong guys. I convinced myself that all the Cosmopolitan magazines were right and it was my right to do what I wanted to do with my body, but it was not until later that I realized the toll that those decisions took on my heart and my self esteem.

The common denominator of my relationships was my desire to be whatever that man wanted me to be, but because I could not be myself, the relationship was doomed to fail.

That marriage was my first abusive relationship, but it was not the last.

My relationships were characterized by physical abuse, verbal abuse, mental and emotional abuse and even sexual abuse.

I went to school and went to work and I went through the motions, but inside the funny, outgoing girl was a broken heart.

In 1986, I ended a nine year relationship and marriage with a man 14 years my senior. I thought I had reached the lowest point of my life.

We had lived together for several years because I wanted to make sure I wasn't making another mistake, but the ink wasn't even dry on our marriage certificate before the dream turned into a nightmare.

He was handsome and charming on the day we stood on a balcony overlooking Birmingham, Alabama and said our vows. But it wasn't long until a new man emerged. He'd never hit me before the wedding, but soon after, many of our "discussions" ended with violence. I quickly learned not to disagree.

When I was "good," he was good and in fact, I was the envy of our friends for having such a caring, romantic husband.

He took me romantic places and bought me expensive gifts. We would wine and dine and life would be wonderful, but in the next moment, he would tell me that everything was terrible between us and it was all my fault! Then he'd want to know what I was going to do to change it! Next would come accusations and threats and I never knew what I'd done that had changed everything.

It was surreal and like living with two different men. I did my best to be good so that the good husband would stay around, but I never could be quite good enough.

Finally, he did not even have to touch me to get me to "behave." A look. A raised eyebrow. A sudden movement or raised hand, and I knew I was in trouble. He was in total control.

On the outside, I was a professional woman with everything going for me. On the inside, I was a total mess because it didn't take a major difference of opinion for this to happen. In fact, the smallest thing would begin the cycle such as grocery shopping at the "wrong store" on the way home from work!

He once threatened to shoot our Labrador retriever puppy that was barking like all puppies do. I begged him to not shoot. He was turned away from me, pointing the gun at the dog and as I cried out, he swung around, pointing the gun at me and very calmly and coolly offered to shoot me instead!

I shut up, the dog stopped barking and we both survived.

Another time, we argued on Easter Sunday after enjoying a wonderful buffet meal with friends. It had rained and as we walked into our bedroom to change out of our dress clothes, he still held an umbrella with a pointed metal tip. I had disagreed with something he'd said at dinner and he began to berate me. In a rage, he shoved me onto the bed, pressing the tip of the umbrella into my throat, threatening to push it through my windpipe. I cowered and apologized for what I'd said and he let me up without hurting me and we went on with our day.

Afterwards, I was shaken and dazed, but he was more loving and charming than ever, acting as if nothing had happened. I began to doubt my sanity.

On the day we married as we drove from the wedding to the reception, he told me that the only divorce we'd ever get would be a .357 Magnum divorce in reference to his favorite gun.

Many times he told me that I could never leave him. That I would spend the rest of my life looking over my shoulder because he would hunt me down and kill me if I left. I believed him.

As a CRNA, I belong to a professional association that keeps licensing records. Many times, I considered leaving, changing my name and giving up my profession for fear he would find me through the association (He was also a CRNA and belonged to the same association. He could be very convincing and charming when he wanted something.). But I knew I'd never be able to go home again to see family and friends and I would live with the fear of him finding me. Once more, I would give up my plans and try to make it work.

Finally, in 1986, I could no longer live with the constant tension and abuse. At first, I planned to run, but I was just too emotionally and physically exhausted. I didn't want to die, but I was too tired to keep living the way I'd been living. I believed there was a good chance that I would end up one of those women you read about in the news who is separated from her husband or lover. When she shows up to work one day, he is waiting with a gun and her life ends splattered in the parking lot. I had looked into a restraining order, but I knew that would not stop him if he decided to come after me. I was so tired of living in fear that I didn't care anymore. I thought "So be it. If that is how it ends, then that is how it ends."

I wasn't moving far away, but I did plan to move out secretly. He got wind of it and showed up when the moving men were there. He bullied them into taking some of my things back into the house. He threatened them and threatened me. Over the next few months, he questioned and bribed enough people until he knew the secure, gated community I'd moved into and my unlisted phone number, but finally, when the bullying no longer worked, he left me alone.

He always told me that no one would ever love me like he did (that was one statement that I'm glad was true!) and that I would always be alone.

Within a few months I was dating, but didn't realize that I was on the rebound and determined to prove him wrong.

I was 30 years old and my biological clock was ticking like a time bomb! I'd hit the snooze button more than a few times, but had begun to think about having children. And about this time I met a man who treated me nicely and wanted to settle down and have children! It seemed to be a match made in heaven.

My daughter was born in 1989 and I thought I'd found everything I was looking for. There were some tensions, but I was committed to making this marriage work. I thought I had done all that I could to make sure of it.

We'd discussed that if there were any problems, we'd go to counseling.

We had agreed before we married that going to church was important to both of us.

We had counseled with the pastor before the wedding. I looked forward to a full life with family, true love and deep friendships.

My only complaint was the huge time commitment at the hospital that my job required when Lauren was so small. I'd waited so long for a child, I wanted to spend more time at home with her. He worked for himself selling real estate, but let's just say he wasn't an overachiever. Plus he had the freedom I didn't and we began to argue about money and time.

I wanted to work less and buy a smaller house.

He liked our big house with the swimming pool in the good school district, but I resented that it was my long hours that provided the money for the house and our lifestyle.

Things came to a head and he told me he didn't love me. Not only that, he hadn't loved me for two years. Those two years had been the happiest years of my life because I thought I had what I'd always wanted.

I couldn't breathe. His words were like an axe to my heart. I knew we had problems, but I had never doubted that we could work through whatever problems we had because we loved each other. To find out that the previous years had been a lie was my greatest nightmare. He refused to go to counseling and refused to talk about it except for talking about a settlement.

I had said from the beginning that I did not want to be a single parent. That he had to promise me we were committed to working it out. I don't know what changed his mind, but he asked for another chance and I gave it to him, because of Lauren, but there was constant tension. He kept saying I should just "get over it (what he said) and move on," but I no longer trusted him. Finally, we argued and he slapped me. It was the final straw. I would not live with physical abuse again.

And though I knew I could not live like that, I still felt like a total failure for leaving and this time, I had also failed my child.

I truly had reached bottom. My life was a mess and I didn't know how to fix it.

But God is faithful.

I had come to the end of myself and God was there waiting to pick up the pieces.

I was ready for a drink of Living Water.

I joined a great church and threw myself at the foot of the cross begging God to change me, to change my life. And for months I thought God had whispered in the pastor's ear exactly what I needed to hear. It was healing and freeing as God mended my broken heart and filled in the broken places in my life.

Then in 1995, I moved to Atwood, Kansas so Lauren could enjoy the small town life that I'd loved.

It was a wonderful time. My life was full of raising my daughter who was ready to start school, my job, my church and friends.

I was not looking for love, but love found me!

I have always been a very open person.

In fact, almost too open.

If you wanted to know something about me, all you had to do was ask and I'd spill it all. The good, the bad and the ugly!

God had shown me that it was almost pathological. That I would tell all the dirt about myself so that if someone rejected me, I would know it up front. I wouldn't have invested a lot in the friendship and losing it wouldn't hurt so much.

But it was an old habit and hard to break.

I met a nice man through friends and was very quickly, totally honest with him. He didn't reject me immediately, but our friendship grew cold over a few months. It was the first time a man had rejected me because of my past and I'm a quick learner! I decided not to make that mistake again!

Then I met Kary.

I thought I'd been disqualified from the Godly Husband Sweepstakes, because I had failed so many times. How could I ask God for a mate? Then a dear friend quoted James 4:2 where it says, "We do not have because we do not ask," and told me to *ask* if that was the desire of my heart, because God wanted to give me those desires, because I delighted myself in Him! (Psalm 37:4)

That day I prayed and asked God for a godly husband for me and a father for Lauren. I was prayer journaling at the time and I wrote out exactly what I wanted in a husband! Then I continued to pray very diligently and very specifically about it. At the same time Lauren wanted to be in a "real family" and she began to pray for God to give her a dad and a family!

Kary lived 40 miles away and we had friends in common, but we'd never met. He'd been divorced for five years and had recently been praying for God to send him a mate!

My husband is a wonderful guy and we are alike in some ways and the opposite in others! It has made for some fireworks through the years, but I am crazy about him...even when he drives me crazy!

Kary is like the Knights of old. He is a man of great integrity and his word is his bond. I tell him he was born in the wrong century because he would have fit in so well with the Knights of the Round Table and other dragon slayers!

I love his integrity. When he believes in something, he believes it to the bone. He is loyal to the bitter end and would never run out on a friend. I never doubt that he meant what he said to me on March 1, 1997 when we said our wedding vows.

I, on the other hand, have a new and improved idea every 15 minutes and can be blown like a leaf in the wind. I love to be on the cutting edge of everything new!

Life is all about how something "feels" and God has had to school me in the Kim Zweygardt School of Hard Knocks that I need to believe Him, not my feelings. I am stubborn when I think I'm right, which is much of the time and when I believe in something, I will fight to the bitter end. I'm a loyal friend, but I also spent a lot of my adult life running after the "new and improved" when things got tough and I'd learned to move on and make new friends!

He had not dated a lot and had not wanted a divorce and after rebellion, relationship became my middle name! And I had always been the leaver, not the leave-ee.

Kary had lived in the state of Kansas his whole life and most of it in St. Francis, Kansas and I'd gotten out of Kansas as quickly as I could, though God had brought me back a few years before. (I told Kary I'd just wandered in the desert for 40 years looking for the Promised Land and I'd found it when I moved back to Kansas!)

We both were devout Christians. We both were single parents (he had two boys, Jordan and Britt and I had Lauren). Both of us had decided we would not settle for less than God's best. And we both have a very quirky sense of humor.

Kary was given my phone number by a friend, but it took him six months to call me. But he didn't waste any time after that! The first time we talked on the phone the conversation lasted for two and a half hours!

We discovered all we had in common in our faith, in our interests and in our outlook. We both knew God had done something special.

We had our first date and talking in real life was even better than the phone! He was everything I'd been praying for...and a bag of chips!

Then he and the boys took Lauren and me out on a date to the movies! She was so excited that she wore her best Sunday school dress and the boys were polite and so precious, I began to envision a future as a family.

Then began the struggle within my heart. When and where and how much did I tell him about my past?

Then one night he told me he had to talk to me about something serious and asked me how I felt about a man with a "heart condition."

My medical person kicked in and my first question was, "what kind of heart condition?"

The caring girlfriend knocked the medical person out of the way as he told me that he'd been diagnosed with a "ragged heart valve" and might have to have open heart surgery someday. Kary isn't afraid of anything, but that night fear of rejection darkened his eyes as he anxiously waited for my reaction.

I told him it did not matter to me because none of us knows the future so we would cross the bridge of heart surgery if and when it came. His eyes cleared as he grinned from ear to ear and said, "That is such a relief! I wanted to tell you so there are no secrets between us."

Time stopped.

I had been praying for an opening to tell him about my past, and I knew that God had opened the door. In fact, it looked like a door a Mac truck could drive through, but I wasn't ready yet! I argued with God in that moment, but I heard Him say, "Tell him now. If you don't, you never will."

With a deep gulp and many tears, I began to pour out my story to Kary, explaining the why and how of the many mistakes I'd made.

I'll never forget the look of love and compassion in his eyes as he said the most beautiful words I'd ever heard, *"It doesn't matter how you got here, honey. The important thing is that you are here."*

Beloved, I do not know your story.

Maybe it is like mine—filled with bad choices and painful consequences. Maybe you feel disqualified from seeking God because you've failed in the past. Maybe you believe that no one could love you or forgive you after what you've done, after the life you've lived.

Or maybe you didn't have a choice. You were molested or rejected and no matter how many times you try to wash away the pain, it lingers. You feel dirty and believe you can never be clean again. All that talk of being "washed in the blood"[3] and "what can wash away my sin?"[4] is just that. Nothing but talk.

You don't even think about it anymore because it hurts too much. You are just trying to get through your days without any more pain.

Or maybe you walked an aisle at church and fell on your knees before Christ, begging Him to save you. They've said that is all you have to do, but it seems way too easy and you struggle with feeling that you need to do something more.

You're grateful to be saved, but how can he bless someone like you?

Do you feel like you're watching life go by through a window?

Through the window the sun is shining, streaming through billowing clouds in an azure blue sky. Flowers grow in a riot of pinks and purples, yellows and reds just below the window. They are so close and vibrant, you can almost smell their fragrance through the glass.

A soft breeze whispers through the variegated leaves of every kind of tree you can imagine and you would swear the breeze whispered your name. It is comforting somehow.

A white lattice gazebo guards a wicker table and chairs set in a small clearing in the trees. The table is set for two with fine white china. All your favorite foods have been prepared and displayed on serving dishes as if a gourmet cook had come to cook just for you. Crystal glasses are at each place, but they are empty. The white table cloth and napkins are crisp. Everything appears as if it is just waiting for someone to come and dine.

You can see it all clearly through the glass, but surely, it is there for someone else to enjoy. You think it is much too fine for your use.

After all, you live on the other side. Your small plain room is good enough. But you can't stay away from the window, pressing your face against the glass, waiting to see who will come to the table and dreaming of what might have been.

As you watch, the door of your room swings open and the breeze beckons you to come. You walk as if in a dream to the table. A striking looking man appears and pulls back the chair for you to sit down. He looks familiar, but before you can ask if you know him, he picks up the crystal pitcher to pour you a glass of the most deliciously cold sparkling water you have ever seen and offers it to you to drink!

Your first instinct is to push it away. You are sure there has been a mistake. You start to tell him about the other room and why you

STORIES FROM THE WELL   41

were there, but suddenly, you are so thirsty, you cannot help yourself! You have to take a drink!

You gulp a drink of the most refreshing water you have ever tasted, but then shame washes over you. You hand the glass back to the kind man with the eyes so full of life and love. But as you tell him there has been a mistake, he quiets you and says, "It doesn't matter how you got here, Beloved. The important thing is that you are here!"

The woman came to the well that day having disqualified herself from polite society. She came alone to avoid the ones who with every look and snub said they were better than her.

No one had to tell her she was a sinner. She knew she had broken all the rules. She knew her sins had made her the bad girl of Sychar.

What she didn't know was that when Jesus is waiting for you, nothing disqualifies you!

Col. 1:12-13 says we should be "...always thankful to the Father who has made us fit to share all the wonderful things that belong to those who live in the kingdom of light for He has rescued us out of the darkness and gloom of Satan's kingdom and brought us into the kingdom of His dear Son."

Verse 14 goes on to say that the Son bought our freedom with his blood.

Beloved, He doesn't purchase junk! We have been made with value as we were made in the image of God. The Latin's called it the Imago Dei.[5] Others have called being made in His image the fingerprints of God. And if that wasn't enough, He sent His son who made us fit to share the wonderful things of the Kingdom and bought us with his blood so we can live there with him!

It is something that all the muck and mire and wrong choices cannot obscure. It didn't matter how she got to the well or how she had lived until that day when she met Jesus.

What mattered was that she had come to the well and He was waiting. The water was for her! The water is for you!

What are you waiting for?

Drink up!

Father,

I thank you that you don't care how I got here, but that I am here. Teach me Your way, Lord. I am thirsty. Open my ears, open my heart, draw me to You and speak to me in ways that I can understand.

In Jesus' name,

Amen.

"Religion never saved anyone."

Seven

RELIGION DOESN'T BRING LIFE

Julie's eyes sparkled as we drove down the dirt road past the now deserted Catholic church and high school long closed.

As the memories came back and she shared them with us, she laughed again like the teenager she was when she'd attended high school there.

Julie grew up in a large Catholic family that lived on a farm near Norcatur, Kansas. There were many other large families who farmed the rich Kansas soil when Julie was young. They didn't have the many conveniences of farmers today, but there are fond memories of working hard and playing hard, but most important to these hard working families was living their faith.

The rolling Northwest Kansas countryside is dotted with beautiful Catholic cathedrals financed by the faithful, hard working men who were dedicated to the Catholic c hurch, their faith and caring for their families. It was a difficult life and the fellowship of church was a welcome break from the arduous task of making a living in harsh conditions. It was the center of their social life as well as a place for education and worship.

As was the custom, Julie attended Catholic grade school, but the high school was in another town. To continue her education, she boarded with a family in the small town that housed the Catholic high school, traveling home for weekends. Seeing the high school had triggered memories of those good days as we drove by the familiar places now closed.

Julie never questioned her faith. It was just a part of life in her devout family. When two brothers were called to the priesthood, everyone in her family was proud.

Julie was a pretty, gregarious girl with many friends, but she'd developed a special friendship with a handsome young man named Norm.

After graduation she married Norman Gallentine and settled down into the rhythm and routine of other young couples in their small town in Kansas—work, family and church.

Norman worked very hard and was a good provider. Soon babies came along. They had a nice home and Julie was happy and busy being a wife and mom. It was what she'd wanted and she didn't consider doing anything else though women were entering the workplace. Running after children and keeping a home and her family fed left little time to think about there being any more to life than what she knew, but God had another idea.

On an ordinary day, when she had seen Norman off to work and waved good-bye to the children as they got on the school bus, Julie sat down at her kitchen table for another cup of coffee.

The kitchen was warm and comfortable. The coffee hot and comforting. Nothing had happened to make her long for more than what her life had been blessed with. But in Julie's words, as she sat down, she didn't really utter the words out loud and she didn't even say them to anyone in particular, but the cry of her heart was, "Is this all there is? Isn't there more to life than this?"

She wasn't unhappy or dissatisfied with her life, but something deep within her called out to deep and God answered quickly.

Julie had heard about a revival going on in Norcatur. Curiosity led her to the door of that meeting, but something about what she heard there attracted her. She had never been to anything quite like it. There was no liturgy like the church services that she was used to, but God began stirring her heart with the words she heard there. She wasn't aware of it but the God of love had begun to woo her to win her heart.

Not long after that, Julie got a call from a woman she knew inviting her to a meeting of Christian women in Norton.

Julie was curious, but reluctant. It wasn't a Catholic meeting, but she knew some of the women going. She made up her mind she wouldn't go, but something kept nudging her to consider it. To just go once and see what it was all about. She delayed until there wasn't time to get ready, then in a rush changed her mind once more.

Those were the days before wash and wear hair styles and you certainly wouldn't go out without full make-up and styled hair, and Julie was sure she would be too late even as she showered and got ready. Instead, when she looked at the clock after fixing her hair and make-up, it was exactly time to go.

When she got to the meeting, it was very informal and all about having a relationship with Jesus, not following religious rules and regulations.

At that meeting, Julie met Jesus and committed her heart to Him! Not the statue Jesus she'd seen at church. Not a judgmental Jesus from Catholic school, but the Living Christ who had come to seek and save the lost. And for the first time, Julie realized that included her!

She prayed and asked Jesus to come into her heart. She prayed that God would give her all the fullness of eternal life and all of His gifts.

Her spirit was healed and she was filled to overflowing with the Holy Spirit that day.

As Julie said, "It changed everything!" The woman who went home that day was not the same one who had so hurriedly showered and gotten ready that morning. Not only had an inward transformation taken place, you could *see* the difference in Julie and she couldn't wait to tell Norman.

God had been softening Norman's heart as well and as soon as he saw his already bubbly wife, bubbling over, he re-committed his life to following Jesus.

In his youth, Norman had had a "born again" experience where he'd accepted Jesus as his Savior, but he had not been dedicated to living for Him. This time he fully committed his life and their marriage and they have served Him together all these years.

Even with a lifetime of religious teaching, Julie's heart cried for more than just the experience of going to church. When she met Him face to face she *knew* what was different!

Life!

At His call, Julie stepped into the River of Life and in her words, after that day "never looked back!"

When she told me her story a few months ago, the vivid expression on her face and the excitement of her voice told me that she spoke the truth when she said that with the passing years, her love for the Savior has only gotten deeper.

Even though some would consider Julie a "Senior Saint", she giggled like a young girl as she described the difference she'd found in living a life filled with His love. Julie and Norm have learned that life in Christ and being filled with His Holy Spirit is truly the Living Water that Jesus speaks of in John 4.

It is the water that never runs dry.

We don't know anything about the life of the woman at the well before the many marriages and wrong choices, but she questions Jesus about what the Samaritan's believed concerning worship versus the belief of the Jews. She mentions the Messiah who is to come, not recognizing that she is engaged in conversation with Him at that moment!

Surely, she had some religious teaching of some kind.

Was she brought up in a family of believers? Did she attend services at the local synagogue sitting with her mother in the Court of Women? Had her first wedding been a celebration promising to honor God in their union?

When her life fell apart had she turned to the church for answers? Was she been rebuffed and never went back?

Or maybe in desperation, she held onto her religious teaching hoping that some knowledge about God might earn her some brownie points at the judgment.

But religion never saved anyone.

Religion is all about doing the "right thing," following a list of do's and don'ts, hoping you make the cut when it's all been said and done.

My parents taught me right from wrong. But you *did* right because it *was* right, not because you loved God. You did your best and hoped He blessed!

But just like living with my ex husband—you can never be quite good enough, no matter how hard you try.

You see, we are all sinners, in need of a Savior!

The Bible says that all have sinned and fall short of the glory of God! (Romans 3:23)

The woman questioned Jesus about the place of worship still wanting to be right about something.

I believe that though others had long given up on her, though they thought she was way past redemption, she was still looking for a way to be right with God.

"I know that the Messiah is coming, who is called the Christ, and when He comes, He will make everything plain to us."

Can you hear the plaintive cry of her heart?

STORIES FROM THE WELL

47

"If I can just hold on, I can ask Him why my life has been this way! I've asked and asked and done my best and I've still failed. They say I am beyond hope, but what will *He* say? When He comes, will He have the answer? For *me*?"

My heart breaks for her and yet, isn't that the question of all our hearts?

"I've done my best and I still fall short! What will become of me if my best isn't good enough?"

And like Julie, "Is this all there is? Isn't there more to life than this?"

It is the cry of the human heart and the question that has been asked through the ages. "What is to become of me?"

And the answer is the answer of the ages. His name is Jesus!

God knew we couldn't do it on our own. Our shortcomings and failures that God calls "sin" separate us from God. Religion—just trying our best to be good and following the rules and regulations—won't get us back to God.

He sent His son, Jesus, to be a sacrifice instead of us, putting Himself on a cross to die so that we would not suffer the penalty of death for our wrongdoings. He died that we might live, defeating death in His resurrection that we might not have dead religion, but a living relationship with Him!

He died that we might have Life!

He offers each of us Living Water!

He said it best in John 4:14.

"but the water I give him shall be in him a well of water springing up into everlasting life!"

Have you met this Jesus?

Or are you still asking, "Is this it? Isn't there more?"

Don't settle for dead religion.

Splash into the River of Life!

Dear Jesus,

I confess that I have tried to get to God by working hard to be good and doing my best, but I have failed. I am a sinner. I have always fallen short and see now that I can't be good enough. I can't fix myself. Please come into my heart and save me! I believe that You are the Son of God sent to seek and to save the lost. I believe that You died for me and rose again to defeat death. You died that I might have eternal life. Thank you, Jesus! Be my Lord and Savior. Show me how to live, not with dead religion, but in relationship with You! In Your precious name,

Amen.

Congratulations and welcome to the family!

"Are you ready to tell the the truth? Are you ready to accept His Truth?"

Eight

TRUTH = FREEDOM!

From the outside, Kristi Epp seemed perfect. If I'd gone to school with her, I would have thought she was one of *those girls* in high school. You know the ones. You struggle with everything and they seem to do everything well. You'd like to dislike them, but in Kristi's case, you can't because on top of excelling at everything...she's so nice!

But many times outside perfection hides the deep fear of imperfection.

Though long past her student athlete days, when we met she was wearing what I call the cute tomboy look: Sweats and tennis shoes, but blonde hair styled and piled high on her head in a mass of curls. Kristi still has the intensity of competitive athletics, leaning forward in her chair as we talked about the hard stuff of her life.

Kristi grew up with a charmed life. Pretty, blonde, talented and athletic, Kristi was raised in a good, Christian home where going to church was just the norm. She loved church and Sunday School and learning about Jesus.

But her Christian family was like any family—not perfect. Her mom, Judy, was dealing with her own parenting issues having been raised by a father with an alcohol problem. And Judy had given her first baby up for adoption which colored every relationship in the family as she struggled with the loss of that child..

Kristi remembers mostly happy times in the family, but she came through her childhood deeply insecure for whatever reason.

She accepted Christ as her Savior when she was around six years old. She understood what she was doing and remembers it clearly, but somehow, even knowing that Jesus was the friend that sticks closer than a brother didn't relieve the insecurity that she felt.

In her head, she knew that her family loved her. She heard the words, but they seemed empty at best. She listened in church to the descriptions of God's love, but all she could see were her own shortcomings. She'd sit, pristine and all dressed up in the pew with her family, wondering why He would love someone as imperfect as she was.

Junior and senior high school brought greater and greater involvement with sports and sports became Kristi's life. She loved the cheering of the crowd and the team work of playing competitive sports. On the court, she could forget she wasn't good enough because for the minutes of the game, she was as good as she needed to be. She was well known by the fans, but even the accolades for all the things she did well didn't wipe out the nagging voice that she had made mistakes and she wasn't worthy of all the attention. Perfectionism had reared its ugly head.

Boys soon noticed the athletic, vivacious blonde teenager and dating became a part of her search for significance. Though she knew the Bible taught it was wrong, the longing to have the empty places within her filled by someone who loved her won out and she lost her virginity at age 15.

But teenage romance is often short lived and that boy was followed by others. And even the temporary pleasure and thrill of sex could not fill the void within her.

Kristi was on a merry-go-round that she didn't know how to stop. Judy saw her repeating the destructive choices and tried to talk to her, but Kristi wouldn't listen. The drive within her that kept her looking for love was greater than the voice of her mom or even the voice of God.

Kristi believed that she was too far down the path of wrong to turn around and turn to God. Too much pain. Too many bad decisions. Too much sin to let God love her.

Finally, she was sure she'd found true love and married. The marriage failed. She married again and that marriage ended in divorce as well.

During this same time, she was diagnosed with an incurable sexually transmitted disease that ended her days in the locker room and her athletic career.

The thing that was most a part of her identity was no more. God had brought her to the end of herself and she had no place else to turn. Kristi describes it as a time where she was holding her breath, waiting to exhale. Finally, she did breathe again, gulping in the fresh air of God's love.

Over nine months, she and Judy mended their relationship. She reconnected with family and friends. She reconnected with God. Kristi has remarried and has a confidence in her husband that when they said their vows, he meant what he said. She has a happiness that she never thought would be hers. More importantly, she has made her peace with God and who she is in Him.

Kristi says that her confidence is now in the Lord.

She still struggles to see herself as He sees her, but she has learned to refute the lie of the enemy of her soul that tells her there is something missing or that God will disappoint her.

How did she come to this place?

When Kristi had run away from God and could run no more and He caught her at the end of herself, she told Him the truth. And He spoke His Truth to her. Speaking to her heart, answering her deepest longing and need.

Why she didn't believe Him the first time, I don't know.

Maybe she was too young or maybe the voice of the world was louder than the still small voice of God, but finally Kristi heard His voice call her name.

Just like the woman at the well that long ago day in Samaria.

When Jesus told her the Truth about Himself, she believed.

"The water I give will become a well of water springing up to eternal life!"

Something in the way He said it, she knew it was True! And even more, she knew it was for her!

Can you imagine how her hope and joy turned to ashes when she asks for the water and it seems that Jesus changes the subject? What she has been looking for is within her grasp and then is seemingly snatched away?

"Go. Get your husband and come back."

All of heaven waited as the seconds stretched out into eternity.

She had surely lied to herself about her life.

"Marriage? Just a piece of paper. Doesn't prove we love each other."

Possibly she'd lied to others.

"Living together? Where did you get that idea? Well, I don't care what you say, I know the truth!"

Were the lies easier than the whispers?

We don't know, but we *do* know that Jesus wasn't just making polite conversation. It was a turning point for her and the angels held their breath.

"I have no husband."

Four words that changed her life for eternity. I can only imagine the excitement within Jesus as He spoke to her so gently.

"You speak the truth," He said, "when you say you have no husband, for you have had five husbands and even now the man you live with is not your husband."

The Bible tells us, "A bruised reed, he will not break. A smoldering wick, he will not snuff out." (Isaiah 42:3)

She was so fragile. She'd worn the shame of her life to the well that day, putting it on just as she did every day much like the heavy cloak that shielded her from the sun. And she was so weary of wearing it.

Maybe like Kristi, God brought her to the end of herself and she was finally too tired to pretend anymore.

Have you ever tried to teach your child a lesson where you want him to "get it" without driving the point home?

You carefully ask questions guiding the conversation toward what is true. You know he knows, but you want *him* to get it for himself, not have to lecture him again!

Your excitement builds as you get closer and closer to the conclusion. Anticipation grows within your heart as you coach and coax him silently. "You can do it! You know this!" Your expectation grows even greater and you can barely hide your smile as he finally says what you've been waiting for! He gets it and you want to do a dance for joy!

Beloved, don't you think that is how Jesus felt when the woman stopped hiding and told the truth?

Don't you know there was a dance of joy in heaven as Kristi turned *to God* instead of running away from Him?

That heaven rejoiced with Jesus when Kristi told the truth about herself and the lies she'd believed and traded them in for *His Truth* about herself?

So it is with us.

What lies have *you* believed?

Maybe they are not a salvation issue. Maybe they *are* a life issue.

Is there a sin you struggle with, but have convinced yourself that it's too big to overcome?

God is calling you to leadership, but you've disqualified yourself because of what you've done.

God calls you "Beloved" and you're sure He's got the wrong number! I mean, "God is love and all that, but how can He really love me with all I've done?"

Are you smarter than God?

More powerful?

Wiser?

More righteous?

I can hear you laughing now!

"Of course not!" you say. "That would be silly of me!"

But when you believe the lie instead of what God says about you, you are, in fact, saying that God is wrong and you know better!

Oops!

Are you ready to tell the truth?

It won't be easy, but it will be worth it. It is the way to the waters of Life, but there are some things you must learn first about telling the truth.

1) You must know the Truth!

The Bible is a life manual!" It is full of God's words about lots of stuff and is a practical guide and a love letter to us all in one!

But if we don't know what it says, how can we live by it?

For example, I once knew some very nice people who lived a good life including going to church. But they never read God's word for themselves! So they would say things like, "Well, like the Bible says, 'A stitch in time saves nine!'" If you don't know, it *doesn't* say that! (They'd heard it often and thought it was true, and therefore came from the author of Truth! It didn't!)

But He *is* Truth and cannot go against His word, so it's a good thing to know for yourself what it says! Get a good study Bible, one you can understand, then pray and ask God to help you learn from it! Seek out a good Bible teaching church and attend regularly. Be a Truth seeker!

2) Believing Truth is a choice we make.

Satan will always lie to us. It was his first trick in the garden of Eden and he hasn't quit lying since.

So you can't believe anything except what God says. So when you know God's truth from the Bible, *choose* to believe it!

I know that *sounds* simple, but sometimes we make decisions based on how we feel or what someone says or maybe take a poll among our ten best friends about what they think we should do and forget that God's truth is always the authority (even if it doesn't make sense to us or we don't particularly like what it says! For example, I love to eat, but gluttony is a sin! I wish He hadn't listed it as such, but that doesn't change that He said it. My life should line up with His truth, like it or not!)!

Jeremiah 17:9 says, "The heart is deceitful above all things and beyond cure. Who should know it."

That sounds pretty harsh, but God is giving us a warning here.

We filter all of life through our perceptions. How we see the world is based on how God designed us, the family we grew up in, the hurts and joys we've experienced, the teaching we've received. All of these things color our world for good or for bad!

Have you ever known two people who could be in on the same conversation and come away with two totally different perceptions of what was said?

My husband and I do it all the time!

That is why we cannot rely on what we think and feel unless we are lined up with God's truth!

His truth is always the trump card!

3) You must <u>tell</u> the truth.

The Bible says "Then you will *know the Truth* and the *Truth will set you free*" (John 8:32). (emphasis added)

Well, if that is true, then why are there so many liars?

We all do it…if we're honest!

From, "Honey, does this make me look fat?" to "No, I don't mind if you play golf this Saturday!" (Big smile followed by the silent, "even though you promised me we'd clean out the garage!")

Or how about, "I'm sorry I'm late, Mr. Smith!"

"Traffic jam?"

Smile and nod, congratulating yourself that you didn't actually *tell* a lie.

"If that is the impression he got, well, that's not my problem."

Again, we must go to the word of God and choose to do things His way.

You see, it is a life or death matter.

The Bible says that life and death lie in the power of the tongue. (Prov. 18:21)

And James 3:6 says, "The tongue also is a fire, a world of evil among the parts of the body. It corrupts the whole person, sets the whole course of his life on fire, and is itself set on fire by hell."

Gulp! It says it right there. If we continually choose to lie, we are choosing sin and death.

Both Kristi and the woman at the well had a choice to make when lovingly confronted by God.

They could tell the truth and accept His gift. Or they could cover up their sin by heaping lies on top just as Eve did in the garden when she made herself a covering of leaves to hide her shame.(Gen. 3:7)

But there are other creative ways to hide from God.

Sometimes lying is making excuses.

I could tell the Lord that my colorful marital history is because I didn't know better or had a bad example of marriage in my home or from childhood abuse when I was fondled by a family friend.

There is an element of truth in all those stories and the Lord knows it. For years, I played the victim and shielded myself against His truth by holding onto those excuses for my sin.

But the Lord also knows my heart. He knows that I became fond of my sin and wanted to go my own way. He knows I ran and hid from Him and pretended that I didn't know what I was doing was wrong. He knows that I willfully made many sinful choices and sinned against Him, myself and others.

And that is the truth.

It is what I had to confess to Him when He brought me to the end of myself and when I did, I heard Him say, "All right. Now we're getting somewhere!"

He loved me too much to let me hold onto the lies! Only when I tell Him the truth about myself, can I accept the Truth of who He is!

Only when I tell the truth about my sin can He cleanse me from it.

Only when I tell His Truth can I live a transformed life.

Nancy Leigh DeMoss[5] says that it is not crazy to talk to ourselves when we are needing someone to tell us the truth! As long as the Truth we're telling ourselves is GOD'S Truth!

It's so true! Only when I tell His Truth do I dive into the River of refreshing, cleansing, life-giving, Living Water!

In Kristi's words, there is nothing like experiencing the awesome love of God! With tears streaming down her face, she said, "You can't get it from here," gesturing to encompass the world.

She had tried everything to find love, traveling many wrong roads on her quest for acceptance. Along the way, she hurt herself and others. Her life is now dedicated to telling her story. It is raw and often shocking, but it is the Truth. And it has set her free!

Are you ready to tell the truth? Are you ready to accept His Truth? Heaven is waiting...

Dear Lord,

I thank You that You are Truth! Forgive me for believing the lies of this world both big and small. I know that all of them lead me further from You. Sometimes I lie to hide from the truth. I lie to make myself look better than I am. I lie because I don't want to hurt others or be hurt myself. I lie because I am ashamed.

I confess to You that I am hiding behind the lie just as Eve hid in the Garden.

Father, help me to be a Truth-teller. First of all, bring to my mind my sins so that I might confess them to You.

Thank You for Your forgiveness, Lord. Thank You that no one is beyond Your grace, when we tell You the truth about ourselves!

Help me to speak the Truth in love to myself and others. Help me to believe what Your word says about You, life, myself and others. Give me a heart and longing for the Truth of Your word and lead me in paths of righteousness.

Lord, use me to show Your Truth to others.
In Jesus' name,
Amen.

"God is at work even in the daily-ness of our lives."

Nine

NATURAL NEED—
SUPERNATURAL ANSWER

I have known Vonnie Oaks for 24 years and still remember the first time I saw her. Vonnie has a way about her that you don't forget. We didn't really say anything of significance that first day as she and Carl carried things into their apartment and I came home with the heavy stack of medical books that was my constant companion in those days of anesthesia training.

I had always wanted to live in a ground floor apartment instead of schlepping my books and groceries up and down flights of stairs and I was thrilled to be living at ground level in Mountain Top Apartments in Birmingham, Alabama.

Vonnie and Carl moved in right above me as my upstairs neighbors, but soon after they moved in, I learned the downside of being down-stairs was hearing all the noise from upstairs!

Vonnie loves to dance. The South Carolina Shag, Appalachian Clogging, all of it was fun for this friendly, funny woman.

My china was trembling in the hutch and the chandelier was swinging when I politely went upstairs and asked them to keep it down a little! I was in school and trying to study!

They were friendly and apologetic and we soon exchanged dinner invitations. We became fast friends.

Vonnie is a strikingly beautiful woman with a sweetness that draws you deep into her eyes and somewhat mysterious smile.

She and Carl were obviously crazy about each other. I loved her naivety and fresh outlook on life.

It was a time in my life where I either worked, studied, or partied. I was far away from the Lord and was living with the man who would become my most abusive husband. Vonnie and Carl were also living together, so we had that in common. Most of our conversations were no deeper than where to have dinner, but God works in mysterious ways!

By 1986, I had ended the abusive marriage and Vonnie and Carl had married and moved to Knoxville, Tennessee.

The Lord was beginning to deal with me about my life when I went to visit them. They were in a place of life change as well. Suddenly, our friendship deepened based on our growing faith. Through the ups and downs of my life, they were encouraging. Instead of where to go eat, we discussed the things of God. They accepted and loved me no matter where I was on the path of my life.

After I moved back to Kansas, it was harder to get to Tennessee to visit and I hate to say it, but for many years we lost touch. It was busyness and life changes, not any problem or misunderstanding, but I missed them. On a recent trip to Tennessee, we had a chance to reconnect.

It was like old times. We did talk about how we met and funny things that had happened, and we caught up on what had ensued in the years we'd lost touch, but mostly, we started up where we left off. There was a level of comfort that only comes with long friendship and a level of deep sharing can only come from hanging out with the same person...Jesus!

When I told them I was writing this book, Vonnie e-mailed me briefly about her first drink of living water and how it changed her life.

Here is her e-mail:

"Kim: You know my life story about a 'life changing event'. But in a nutshell "I was scrambling through life determined I could do it ALL ON MY OWN. Never thinking seriously about a "Life Partner". Then on a very regular day, a very caring man & I had a chance encounter. That was the day I very tearfully & humbly started praying for guidance to find my life partner. That, too, was the day I lost interest in flirting, dating, etc. I was smitten. We didn't know about each other's response to that 1st day of "Love @ 1st sight" until months later. But long story short—we have walked and prayed together ever since. (26 years) I'll always believe that my turning to prayer that day in response to my feelings of true love for a man was what altered my life."

A few years ago they started a business that has made them very successful and they recently moved into a beautiful home on a golf course outside of Knoxville. She goes on, "Today is moving day—closed yesterday. Yesterday was unexpectedly emotional—several different times—the tears just began to fall. I never in my wildest dreams would have expected to live in such a beautiful home with my sweetheart. Tonight we'll spend the 1st night there. We had our 1st meal there yesterday @ lunch—McDonald's—even saying grace over our burgers brought a downstream of tears. Wow."

Vonnie was like many of us. Young, brash, thought we had the world by the tail. And we thought that whatever came our way, we could handle it.

Sometimes life takes an unexpected turn. Sometimes it takes a tragedy or "near miss" to change our lives. But God is at work even in the daily-ness of our lives.

For Vonnie, it was a chance encounter in a stairway at work that changed her life and brought her to her knees.

We all love the great salvation stories! Drama! Danger! Going to Hell in a hand basket!

The man who didn't jump from a balcony when he heard a voice call his name and was sure it was God. The man walking in a fog that cried out a name he didn't know in response to a nudge from God. Divine Appointments! Great stories of faith!

But God uses even the mundane to call us. And when we admit our need, He is there, ready to welcome us home!

Vonnie wasn't looking for God. She was looking for true love! But God Himself *is* love. He used the desire of her heart to soften her heart to Him.

She realized a need and prayed.

God was listening and began to answer her prayer.

Through a small incident, she became aware of God working in her life, of His love for her though she was not living for Him. He gave her a sip of refreshing water, making her long for a deeper drink.

Change didn't come immediately. Even as God answered her prayer, she didn't change overnight. But God continued to woo her until she turned fully to Him!

In every great story there is a climax, a turning point upon which the story hinges.

So it is with this love story. Vonnie could have flirted and connived and come up with a way to interest Carl, but instead, she admitted her need to the only One who could fill it!

It seems backwards doesn't it? Wouldn't you think the way the story *should* be written is that Vonnie realizes she needs God, prays to accept Jesus as her Savior and, as a reward, God gives her Carl?

That is the way I'd do it if I were God...but I'm not God!

In His love for her, He took the small thing she offered Him—her recognition that she couldn't do this on her own and needed His wisdom—and blessed it out of His love for her.

He desires to give good gifts to His children! (Matt. 7:11)

That long ago day at the well, the woman stood uncertainly, wondering what this man was all about.

Jesus had said, "If you knew the gift of God, and who is saying to you, 'Give me a drink', you would have asked him and he would have given you living water."

At that moment, the woman didn't even know she was looking for a Savior. Sure she knew her sinfulness, but she was doing the best she could. At some point, much like Vonnie, she'd decided that she could do it all on her own.

Jesus had said, "If you knew the gift of God..." and she didn't. She knew *about* Him. She knew about her religious heritage and argued with Jesus about where to worship, not realizing that God stood before her!

It is human nature to problem solve and then continue to do what we think works to make it in life.

But Jesus brought her to recognition that he's offering her something she *cannot* supply for herself. Before she takes the Living Water, she must admit that she *needs* what He is offering!

Jesus said, "He who drinks of this water will get thirsty again. But whoever drinks from the water that I will give him will never get thirsty again—ever!"

Suddenly, she sees something that she does not have. She has been to this well over and over to drink her fill, she'd taken water home to quench her thirst. But nothing changed! She must always return for more water. Her thirst is never satisfied.

The woman's story really begins in the next verse when she tells Jesus she wants the water He has offered to her.

Please, please, Beloved, don't confuse this with Salvation!

Though the woman was at the point of meeting Jesus as her Savior, He offered her *Living Water.*

When we enter the Kingdom of God nothing can snatch us out of His hand. We are secure!

But Living Water is something more.

It is not a one-time offer!

He plainly says, "that you might *never* thirst again!"

That is ongoing!

That is life changing!

It is being transformed into the image of Christ!

Let me ask you, how often do we need water?

Scientists say we can go without food for days, but we *must* have water!

Some places in Scripture, Jesus calls himself the Bread of Life.

I like that.

We need food and bread is a life sustaining food.

And even as the disciples return to Jesus in John 4:31, they offer Jesus food. But He says, "I have food you know nothing about."

Yes, food is great, and Jesus offers that too, but *water?*

Water is a precious, life-sustaining commodity.

Ask anyone in a Third World country how precious is pure water.

Ask those living in drought stricken nations how precious is a drop of water.

And he offered this most valuable and precious gift of water, abundant and life sustaining, to this woman.

And as He offered her something she knew she needed in the natural, she recognized her need, first in the natural and then in the supernatural.

"Don't despise small beginnings," said the prophet Zachariah! (Zach. 4:10)

You have come to Him for eternal life, but He has lots for you on this side of eternity as well!

Has God given you a dream, but you don't see any way it could come true?

Do you long to make a difference in the world, but you're just one person?

What is it?

Feeding the hungry or leading a Bible Study?

Maybe there is a relationship that needs restored, but you've been rebuffed so many times, you think, "What's the use?"

Maybe your marriage is not all you dreamed it would be or there is conflict with your kids where once was closeness and you don't know how to bridge the gap.

Do you need to lose weight or stop smoking?

Or your tongue is sharp and you spend as much time eating your words as you do eating chocolate?

You long to be like Jesus, but you don't know where to start.

Or maybe you are uncertain about the claims of Christ and aren't sure you even want all that Christ offers.

Maybe you've wanted to ask, but couldn't bear the disappointment if all this God stuff isn't true.

You've heard Him call your name, but didn't know how to answer.

Would you ask one more time?

Would you take a risk that what the woman found at the well could be true for you, too?

Could you take a risk like Vonnie and admit that there is something you want or need that you can't do on your own?

You don't have to want all that God offers today. You just have to "want to want to."

Get it?

What is your need in the natural? Can you ask Him for it? Admit that you need it?

Now I'm not saying ask for a million bucks or to win the lottery. That is not your need.

But do you need to feel safe? Do you need love? Are you lonely and need a friend? Need a place to stay or a warm meal? Are you sick and in need of healing? Do you lack faith to even believe that all this God and Jesus stuff is real?

Ask Him. It begins with admitting you don't have the answers and can't do it on your own. Let Him do the rest.

In Mark 9, Jesus finds his disciples with a boy who is demon possessed. A large group of people had gathered around and they were arguing because the disciples had been unable to cast out the demon. The father asks Jesus "if you can do anything to help us, take pity on us."(Mark 9:22b New Life Version)

Jesus says, "If You can? All things are possible for those who believe!"(Mark 9:23 NIV)

I can hear you asking, "But, Kim, what do I do if I *don't* believe?"

STORIES FROM THE WELL 63

Beloved, follow the example that was written for us to follow!
Mark 9: 24 tells us how the father prayed a simple, honest prayer.
"I believe, Lord. Help my unbelief."
He *wanted* to believe and had enough faith to *ask* for more.

The woman who walked to the well that day thought she was out of
faith, that she'd fallen short in the belief department.
After all, hadn't she believed that it would all work out somehow?
(Does it not take faith in *something* to marry five times?) Didn't she
believe that somehow, someway, she could make it work? Didn't she
scramble through life just as Vonnie did, convinced that if she tried
hard enough, life would all work out for her?
But her life never changed until she admitted her need to the only
One who could answer the question she'd been asking with every fail-
ure. "Doesn't anyone care that I am thirsty?"
He does.
And after you ask, don't forget that God shows up in unexpected
places!
It may be a chance encounter on a mundane day that changes everything!

Dear Lord,
I admit that in so many ways, I've tried to get through life on my own.
Right now my faith is weak. I am not sure that You can meet my needs,
but I am willing to ask. I admit that I need a refreshing just like the
woman at the well. Lord, I need...(list what you need). Lord, help me
to see you at work in my every day. Thank you in advance for answer-
ing my prayer.
In Jesus' name,
Amen.

One glass of Living Water coming right up!

"That night it was as if God Himself had rejected her."

Ten

THE ANSWER FROM AN UNLIKELY SOURCE

Listening to Kacy's story was painful, but oh, so familiar to me.

Not her circumstance, particularly, but the way she talked about herself, her life and her pain in third person, detached from the story, almost as if she was telling the deep hurtful story of someone else with whom she had no connection.

I've been there. Shut off from the emotions associated with the agonizing pain of life, but with the need to tell someone, anyone, in hopes it makes a difference. That my pain was not wasted and I was not without redemption.

Only as Kacy's story of rebellion and rape unfolded and the tears flowed like a waterfall down her face, did the Kacy of the story become the Kacy telling the story.

Kacy is Kristi's sister. In her own words, her sister Kristi was "the pretty and skinny one" and she was the "dumb one who didn't fit in."

Like her sister, the day we talked Kacy was dressed in sweats, a t-shirt and athletic shoes. But instead of looking like a former athlete, she seemed to be hiding in the bagginess of her clothes, wearing the big t-shirt untucked over her pants.

Kacy's brown hair is cut short with a no-nonsense flair and when thinking or agitated, she runs her hands through it leaving it in spikes. I imagine her going into the beauty shop saying, "Just cut it! Any way! Just so I don't have to mess with it!"

Part of it may be that Kacy is constantly on the run wearing the many hats of wife, mother and student. She is in constant motion giving the impression of being impatient to move on to the next thing. Though she was patient with the interview, I don't think sitting still to chat is a part of her make-up.

Kacy's no-nonsense hair reflects her personality. Her answers to my questions came like rapidly, like gun-fire from an automatic weapon. She seemed eager to tell her story, wanting to get it right and make sure I understood.

It was a painful story. A story of lost hope and recovery. A story of God making everything beautiful in His time.

Though she described herself as being dumb and not fitting in, Kacy didn't always feel that way.

Kacy's earliest memories are of family and friends, going to church and "being a model Christian kid."

She remembers the exact day at Vacation Bible School when she accepted Jesus as her Savior and the feeling that it brought her that she was "good."

Her childhood was pretty normal for a Christian family according to Kacy, but the Epp family moved a lot through Kacy's jr. high and high school years. With the physical and hormonal shifts of puberty and trying to make new friends, Kacy's emotions felt like a roller coaster. She'd always been the happy-go-lucky little girl, but not fitting in made her feel worthless.

Puberty is normally a time of fickle emotions and in Kacy's mind, she had a "Love/Hate" relationship with church. She knew it was the right thing to do, but at an age when she wanted to make her own choices, Kacy felt she went to church because she *had to.* It wasn't so much anything that was said, but Kacy got the feeling that she'd be in really big trouble with God and in trouble with her family if she didn't go to church.

Judy, Kacy's mom, was present at the interview and she disagreed that Kacy would have been in trouble for not going to church through those years, but in Kacy's young mind, "you had to be in church or you'd be in trouble" so she went regularly.

As they had entered junior high, the normal closeness of her relationship with her sister, Kristi, had turned into sibling rivalry. As Kacy grew more self-conscious about her appearance, she became more conscious of Kristi's blonde good looks. Kristi seemed to have it all and she was jealous. But even as her feelings of competition deepened, church was her refuge. It was the place she was a good Christian girl, where she knew God loved her and so did her friends at church.

All of that changed one night at a youth event. Kacy was used to being teased about her appearance from other kids, but this time it came from an unexpected source. In front of the group, the Youth Pastor "jokingly" called her all the names she hated, then turned away, leaving her to fend for herself with her peers. It was excruciatingly painful. She'd heard the words in her own mind a million times as well as heard them from others. She knew the sting of being left out of the popular crowd, but that night it was as if God Himself had rejected her.

Kacy decided, if that was "church"—if that was "God", she wanted no part of it.

Her family didn't know what had happened to her as she left the "right road" for the road of rebellion. In Kacy's memory, she "went into her room and stayed there until graduation." She withdrew from all the things she loved and her parents didn't know how to bridge the gulf that separated them.

When she was 18, the first guy who was attracted to her became her first lover. But the thing that she'd desired to feel loved and important instead deepened her feelings of worthlessness. The minute it was over, she knew she'd made a mistake. She condemned herself for it, but couldn't take it back. She sank into even deeper self loathing for what had happened and felt even more unloved than before.

She turned to alcohol. And paradoxically, to other men. But bad choices breed bad choices and she was betrayed again by someone she trusted who said he cared for her.

Kacy shrugged as she told me, "He did care for me—he just cared for his other girlfriend more."

Kacy was devastated, but things were about to go from bad to worse. She was in a downward spiral of self loathing and bad choices, but the event that almost destroyed her last shred of self esteem was still to come.

One night Kacy was at a party with a group of friends when she *became* the party and was gang raped by five men.

Her self esteem was so damaged that she blamed herself for being there and at first told no one. That event triggered Kacy's slide into the depths of hell that lasted five to six years.

The happy little girl who loved Jesus became spiteful and mean. She was so angry that she fantasized of killing the men who'd hurt her. Her moods swung between depression and rage. She turned the rage inward and considered suicide a welcome escape. Alcohol became her best friend since being drunk dulled both pain and memory and she could forget the rape for a brief respite.

But if she was angry about the rape, she was angrier still with the youth pastor who'd rejected her and the God he represented. In Kacy's words, "God was not who He said He was."

It was the age old question. "Where was God when this happened and why didn't He do something about it?"

The rage and alcohol did nothing to heal her. Instead it fueled the fire of hurt and hopelessness that raged within her. Her anger and mood swings had alienated both family and friends who couldn't understand the erratic moods and hurtful words Kacy spewed at everyone close to her. Suicide became more than a consideration and Kacy tried to kill herself, but miraculously survived.

In the midst of this, God brought a messenger of His love to bring Kacy hope.

It was her 21st birthday when her uncle came to see her, bringing a gift. He was the only member of her family she considered a friend.

He'd had a tough life and did not seem put off by Kacy's lashing out at those closest to her. He'd been raised in an alcoholic home and drank heavily himself so he understood Kacy's demons. He was a man subject to depression who eventually committed suicide, but on that day, God used him to speak to a young girl that even those closest to her would have said was beyond being reached with God's love and grace.

Florists have made a fortune selling bouquets of red roses because they speak the language of extravagant love that we long to hear.

On the birthday that we traditionally celebrate adulthood and coming of age, her uncle brought her one dozen long stemmed red roses. To a young woman who felt older than her years, who considered herself "used goods," the implication of that gift was not lost.

But beyond the roses, he brought her an even greater gift.

"Kacy, the only person who can really love you is God."

Whoosh! The Living Water flooded her parched and weary soul, washing away the mantra of the enemy.

"You worthless idiot, you're used goods, nobody wants you!"

The enemy had whispered it to her in quiet moments and shouted it above her own voice when she tried to refute it.

"Kacy, the only person who can really love you is God."
It was the beginning of her journey home.

All journeys begin with a single step and that includes the journey into the arms of a loving God.
The woman at the well had been mistreated by both men and women in her life.
Most likely she'd been betrayed more than once.
In that culture, women had no rights and when a man wrote out a certificate of divorce, the relationship was ended. It didn't even have to be for a good reason. Just his reason.
Burn the dinner?
Didn't please him?
Didn't bear children or bore children of the wrong sex?
Talked too much?
Lost your looks?
A myriad of small mistakes added up to being unwanted and on the street.
A woman could find herself alone.
Betrayed. Ostracized.
Without hope or help.
Feeling like "used goods."
Until hope comes from an unexpected source.

The Bible says that Jews didn't associate with Samaritans (John 4:9b). An old religious dispute over the place to worship led the Jews to think the Samaritans were little more than animals.
And the Scripture records the woman's almost belligerent tone as she asks, "What? You are a Jew, and you ask me for a drink—me, a Samaritan!" John 4:9a (James Moffatt, New Testament Translation)
We all struggle with being unfairly judged.
Have you heard the phrase, "Life is hard, but God is good?" My daughter and I recently had a long talk about life not being fair.
Lauren is a lovely girl who loves God with her whole heart. But injustice really bugs her! She wants to fight for the underdog and sometimes gets involved with things not really her business!
I laughed as I described her as a 5 foot 5 inch, 119 pound fairness meter! She gets indignant when people don't play fair. She is light-hearted most of the time, but unfair treatment really makes her mad!
Most of us are like that. Life is supposed to be fair, we think, and when it isn't, we're not happy about it!

For women, and especially this woman, life in Samaria was just not fair. She is immediately on the defensive with this upstart Jew who asked her for a drink.

So what was up with her?

Maybe she was just a grouch. Maybe she wasn't nice at all and no man could live with her. Maybe what she said to Jesus was just the tip of the iceberg when it came to her sharp tongue.

It's a possibility.

But I think it more likely she was like the little puppy I bought Lauren when she was three.

Bingo was a tiny Pekingese about the size of Lauren's favorite stuffed lamb and got much the same treatment!

His tail was a perfect handle for carrying him around the house! After only a few days of being loved a little too much, Bingo began to nip at Lauren any time she got near him and Bingo, to Bingo's relief, found a new home soon after.

Bingo didn't start out a mean puppy, but he learned to keep Lauren at arm's length and himself from harm's way.

So it is with us.

The old saw says, "Fool me once, shame on you. Fool me twice, shame on me!"

God designed our physical bodies to take care of vital functions first.

For example, if you have massive bleeding, blood is sent away from the non-vital places like skin and bone to your heart and brain where it really counts.

We do the same thing in our spirits. We learn to guard our heart from non-physical pain. We sense hurt coming and like the porcupine, all our quills go out to keep the predator from getting close enough to hurt us.

So it was with this woman. Even if this woman was always hateful and mean, I would guess she'd learned to protect herself from the things and people who hurt her. Like Kacy, spewing anger and bitterness kept everyone at arms length.

I am sure that the people of Sychar thought she was too far gone for help or hope. She certainly wasn't a "good person" and yet, even after her animosity, when a weary traveler asked her for something, she didn't say no.

Jesus asked her for something simple and within her power to give. "Give me a drink."

And with that request, she engaged what the stranger had to say.

She well understood the need for water in that desert place, but Living Water? Who had heard of such a thing?

She *had* to come to the well for water. It was necessary to sustain life. And it was woman's work.

But she was in a no-win situation.

As lonely as she was, if she came with the other women, she had to endure their snide remarks.

If she came alone, she endured the loneliness, every solitary step branding her an outcast to any observer.

And as much as she hated the heat and weight and the trip to the well, there was no other way.

But then an offer from a complete stranger. From someone who was also an outcast in her eyes—a Jew!

From him, a way out?

From him, Living Water and no more trips to the well?

Puzzled as she was, it was the proverbial offer she couldn't refuse!

What was it about Jesus that she heard the message behind his words?

What was it about Jesus that allowed her to admit the truth to him when her truth was so painful that she had spent a lifetime running from it?

What was it that stopped the continued spiral from the happy-go-lucky girl of her childhood to a life of more and more of the same?

I think it was because He offered her something that answered her question, "Where is God in all of this?"

And when her heart heard the message, everything was different, just as Kacy heard when God spoke to her through her uncle.

"God is the one person who can truly love you."

Something about the woman attracted men. Maybe she was beautiful. Maybe she was fun and lighthearted before hurt and bitterness stole her joy.

Something had brought five men to marry her and a sixth to share her bed. She was no stranger to the dance between men and women, of that we can be sure.

But I think she may have had the same fairness meter as my daughter!

With every failure, as the men went on with their lives and she was left to fend for herself, her heart cried, "It's not fair!"

She was not looking for another man that day at the well, but she was looking for answers.

And the answer came from an unexpected source.

This stranger was different from any man she had met before.

And when he spoke to her, "I am He (the Messiah) the One speaking to you," she responded to the Truth of His words. She heard the voice of the Father. She recognized the love that He offered her.

And she took the first step back toward the Father's love.

Kacy's story didn't end the day God spoke to her through her uncle. She was drinking heavily with no place to turn. She needed to get sober, but wasn't sure what it would take. The thought ran through her mind that being pregnant and not wanting to harm her baby would be about the only thing that could make her quit the alcohol that numbed the pain of her life.

A month later, she was pregnant.

She considered an abortion, but knew it was wrong. Her mother had given a baby up for adoption, the family living under the shadow of that loss, so she didn't think she could choose that. As she sifted through her options, it became clear; she needed to keep her baby.

As the alcohol fog lifted and the baby grew in her womb, Kacy heard the Lord say that her purpose was to raise her baby to love Him and that is what she has done. She loves being a mom and is now very happily married.

Forgiveness of everything that happened to her at the hands of others has been a process, but Kacy has found her mission attending nursing school so that she can be there in the midst of injustice with other victims of rape or abuse.

When I asked Kacy what message she wanted to communicate to women through this book, she didn't hesitate.

"Last year I read "The Purpose Driven Life" by Rick Warren and through that I realized, I'm not a mistake! God didn't screw up in how He made me! No one can take that away from me. (That's what I want them to know,) No matter what anyone says, you're not a mistake!"

Beloved, like Kacy, He's been speaking to you. Did you miss His voice because the message didn't come the way you thought it would?

Don't forget, in history, God has spoken both through a donkey and a cock that crowed! (Num. 22:1-35, Matt. 26:34)

Can you hear Him say, "I am the only One who will always love you?" Can you hear Him whisper, "You are my Beloved and you are not a mistake!"

Let the Living Water flood your soul!

Dear Lord,

Life gets so busy and I get so caught up in the clamor around me that I cannot hear Your voice. I thank You that You have given us Your word as an example of how You speak. You met the woman at the well at her place of need. You met her away from the clamor of other voices and the city streets. You spoke Your truth to her in a way that she could hear the whole message—the words and the love of the Father.

Lord, I need to hear You now. Meet me in a quiet place that I might hear Your voice. Meet me at my place of need that I might be filled with all I need. Lord, let me hear You speak no matter who You speak through. I need to dwell with You, Lord. Show me the way to a place of refreshing and peace.

In Jesus' name,
Amen.

"there was something about her that had changed."

Eleven

LEAVING THE "OLD" BEHIND

Trish Harkness is one of those people I just don't "get."
She thinks technology is fun! A self-described techno geek, Trish
can unscramble the most complex computer mess without getting
ruffled. It is amazing to someone like me who is mostly computer il-
literate!

We attended a Bible Study together and I was taken by her transparency and love for God. She was new to town, so like ladies do, we
spent some time getting to know our new friend as we studied His
Word.

We were all captivated as each week, Trish brought little Braden
with her and mommied him as we studied. Trish laughed easily and
often and her joy was infectious. Her smile is one that lights up her
fair skin and luminous eyes.

Without self-consciousness, Trish confided that she'd grown up
with a devout Catholic father and a mother who believed that where
you worshipped was not as important as whom you worshiped.

Trish was well on her way to becoming a devout Catholic girl when
God upset her apple cart as a high school sophomore.

For Trish, going to heaven meant being a good enough person to earn your spot behind the heavenly gates. Being good meant going to church every Sunday and on special holidays, memorizing the rosary and prayers that go with it, attending church classes, being good to others, confessing your sins and atoning for those sins as the priest told you to.

In 1993, a crusade ministry came through the small Kansas town where Trish lived and was there for several days. God was at work, but so was the enemy!

In the same week there was a dirt storm that filled the auditorium with sand and a blizzard that threatened to call off the event! (You've got to love Kansas weather, but this seems a little more like a spiritual battle than happenstance to me!)

The Lord called out to Trish that first day, but she resisted. What she was hearing went against what she believed about herself and God. After all, she'd gone to church all of her life! How could this be right?

Finally, on the last day of the crusade Trish walked down the aisle of that auditorium to admit publicly that as good as she was, she wasn't good enough. She was a sinner and only God's grace could save her.

Trish can still easily tick off on her fingers the many reasons she thought she was good enough—straight A student, dedicated participant in special choirs and musical groups, loyal friend, obedient daughter, hard worker, and dedicated church-goer. She'd done all the right things, all the good things, but they paled in comparison for what Christ had done for her! And for the first time, Trish realized it wasn't about being good enough. It was about His grace.

It was the beginning of a new life! Trish was like a sponge and God had provided her best friends father as a mentor to help her understand her new faith.

But there was trouble in paradise. Her dad wasn't sure what to do with his daughter's new found faith. When she asked to attend a non-Catholic youth group with her best friend, things came to a head. It was their first major fight.

Trish's dad finally decided that as long as the activity didn't interfere with classes at the Catholic church, Trish could go. Trish was elated.

And until Trish moved out of the house upon graduation, she attended the Catholic church with her family. She had taken God's commands to heart to honor her father and mother. It is a command with a promise (Eph.6:2) for long life and for things to go well.

Trish and her dad remained close and are close to this day although another argument occurred when she decided to be married in a Christian church instead of a Catholic church! But they resolved their differences and he proudly walked her down the aisle.

Trish has a passionate understanding of God's grace. She has known since the day she chose to accept God's grace and confessed Him as her own that Jesus is her Savior, her Refuge and the One she can count on no matter what.

As much as she struggled accepting that no matter how good she was, she wasn't good enough, once she accepted it, she never looked back.

There have been times since that day in 1993 that Trish has strayed from the narrow way or let life push into her time with Jesus, but never has she gone back to the place where she began, trying to earn her spot in heaven!

She tasted that which brings life and nothing else satisfies. There is no work, no goodness, and no accolade of the world that replaces the awesome gift and grace of God. Trish had an early taste of trying to fill her own jar and that was enough. She knows now it cannot be earned. It is His life, His death, His resurrection and grace that saves. Nothing else.

That day at the well, the woman had come once more to fill her jar and then return home to her daily duties that made her a good "wife" and woman of the house.

Clean the house, speak softly and kindly, wash the clothes and cook the supper.

Do your best to be "good" and maybe God will have mercy on your soul.

Such is the life of trying to be "good enough."

Oh, she had her sins. Everyone knew about them, but can't you see her striving to do enough good to make up for the bad?

It's an awful place to be in.

Beloved. I know because I've been there. Trying to be kind enough and nice enough that I can forget the deceit of my own heart.

Trying to do enough good deeds that the people around me will forget my failures, but they never do.

Thinking constantly about God and His big list of all my wrongs.

Dreading what I call, "God of the Big Hammer."

He's a gruff man with a long, snow white beard who watches everything I do with a scowl. He holds a giant hammer in his hand and every time I fall short, he grins in delight as he conks me on the head! Ouch!

Do you know him? I thought that was God, but it is not.

Did the woman think so too? God was up there delighted to punish every misstep?

She might have, but when she meets Jesus everything changes! The Bible says, "Though your sins are as scarlet, they will be white as snow!" (Is. 1:18)

"What can wash away my sins?"
"Nothing but the blood of Jesus!"[4]

Beloved, can you see her?

Suddenly, she is standing in a river from heaven. A river of many rushing waters and they swirl around her. The River of Life is washing away the sin she has carried like a garment of red. Her eyes are opened by His words and she knows that not only can she *not* be good enough to make up for her sin, *neither can anyone else!*

She laughs with delight and cups her hands to drink the bubbling, dancing water. The water spills over her cupped hands and through her fingers, but it doesn't matter. Unlike the well where she returns each day, unlike the water pot she carries so carefully home, this river does not run dry.

She doesn't have to hoard this water! Each crystalline drop explodes in her mouth and rushes through her heart and soul filling all the broken places.

She wades to the edge and smiles at the man who has brought her to this River of Living Water.

She is clean. Her sins have been washed away.

She is full. No need to fix herself anymore.

She is whole. There is no more brokenness.

Everything has changed.

The sky is bluer. The olive trees greener. The dust which had seemed brown and common under her feet only moments ago now sparkles in the glint of the sun like oh, so many jewels. The timbre of the disciples voices as they climb the path back to the well sounds like a joyous celebration where deep voices flow in endless melody.

"I am loved!" her heart sings!

"Yes, you are, my Beloved," God sings back to her!

Anticipation replaces trepidation and she cannot wait to get back to Sychar! She leaves Jesus standing at the well. She leaves her water jar and the past behind and runs back down the path to the village she had longed to escape from. Instead of hiding her face, she runs house to house to tell everyone that she has met Jesus!

Can you imagine the scene?

The incredulous stares at the woman's excitement.

The puzzlement that the woman who only moments ago had trudged alone, hiding her shame with a chip on her shoulder now laughing and shouting in joy?

The Bible says she told the men.

Isn't that interesting?

She had been an outsider to the women and we know that hurts. Anyone who has ever been last chosen on the play ground or not invited to the birthday party knows the feeling of being on the outside of a circle of friends. But at whose hand had the woman suffered the most?

Men are designed by God as the protectors of womanhood although in our feminist society, that idea is considered a little too quaint and old fashioned for most women.

No one had protected her. She had been used and thrown away by the men of the village and yet with great courage and excitement, they were the first ones to hear the message that the Messiah had come to Sychar.

She told them, "He told me everything I ever did!"

Can you imagine the leers that accompanied that revelation?

But it didn't stop her from walking in the new life Jesus had given her. She had gone to the well to fill her need for water. She met a man different from any man she had met before. They had a spiritual conversation. She knew her religion and she was waiting for the chance to meet the Christ "who would explain everything" to her.

Beloved, don't you have a list of questions for God?

I know I do! Maybe Lauren got her fairness meter from me, but there are some things that have happened to me and those I love and though God has turned them all for good, (Rom. 8:28) I'd still love the chance to ask Him to explain it all to me over a big mug of coffee! (I am hoping that along with the river of Living Water, there will be the Pot of Endless Coffee in heaven!)

I can imagine the woman thinking the same thing.

"I don't know what I ever did to deserve some of this, but when that Messiah guy gets here, I'd love to find out what was up with this!"

Okay, well, that part is my imagination, but we do know she had heard about the Christ who was to come and explain some things to them.

But the first thing she had to do when she realized that she had been speaking to this very Messiah was leave her old way behind and learn a new way of life.

I'd like to think that the woman went home, told the man who'd taken her in about Jesus, he went with her, met the Messiah, recognized his own sin, and married her. They then held Torah studies in their home, had many children and lived happily ever after.

What a great story!

What we do know is that people came to Jesus because of what the woman said.

Some were probably curious and some were probably mean enough that they wanted to warn this traveling prophet about the kind of woman he'd been talking to.

But there was something about her that had changed. Many believed because of the woman's testimony. Many more believed because of what He said as He stayed and taught them.

New life had begun in Sychar!

Trish did the same thing. After hearing God call her name and accepting that she was a sinner saved only by God's grace, she went back to her home and family and shared the "good news." She told her friends the "good news." She was so excited that if you met Trish then or you meet Trish now, you're gonna hear the "good news!"

Trish continued doing many of the things that she had done before, but suddenly, her motivation was different! Instead of earning her way to heaven, she could say with the woman at the well, "Jesus told me everything I ever did!"

Trish's sins were different than this woman, but the common denominator is *both women were doing the best they knew how to do to get through life.*

But it was not good enough.

Trish had been busily earning her way into God's grace and Jesus offered her rest by the River of Living Water. Then she began to honor her father by offering him the same rest.

He has seen what the Living Water has given his daughter and finds joy in the good life that God has blessed her with—eleven years of marriage, a sweet baby boy, family and friends, a great career and in her words, "most importantly, the knowledge that though I do not deserve His grace, He freely gives it nonetheless." She adds, "And He will give it to anyone willing to accept it."

Are you ready to leave your water jar behind and with it, trying to be good enough? It's a dead end street. Instead, drink deeply of the new!

Dear Lord,

Sometimes I go through the motions just because it is what I've always done. Or what I've been taught to do or what I think should work. Lord, I lay down the old ways of my life—my coping mechanisms, my habits, my family heritage, the world's way of dealing with stuff—and say, "You take it, Lord! Show me a new way!"

Lord, I want serving You and others in my life to be a joy, not a burden. Refresh me in Your river of living water that I might not thirst again. Keep me from going back to the old ways of filling my "jar." I want to be so different, Lord, that those I meet, including those I know well, will believe in You because of the changes in me.

Thank You for the work You are doing in me! I thirst because I have tried to fill my thirst with the wrong thing and all I really want is what You offer! Thank You for filling me!

In Jesus' name!

Amen.

"Weeping may last for the night, but joy comes in the morning." Psalms 30:5

Twelve

WALKING A NEW PATH

Judy Epp is a pretty, dark-haired, animated woman who is just-the-facts honest.

Her quick smile and laugh attracted me immediately, but as I got to know Judy, her transparency about her own struggles made me want her as a friend. She is one of those people that we all need in life. Someone willing to tell you the hard truth when you need to hear it.

Judy and I had talked on the phone several times as she and her husband planned an all night lock-in for New Year's Eve 2005. She was passionate about young people hearing the message of Christ and I liked that. But I didn't know how passionate, until I saw her dunk her head into a vat of...well, you don't really want to know...on purpose! It was the event's take on Fear Factor and on a dare, Judy was a participant.

Wow! I thought, "This woman means business!"

It was just one example of how dedicated and willing Judy is when it comes to kids and the Gospel!

Hard as it is to believe, Judy wasn't always this way. When I asked for stories for this book, she replied immediately and offered her story. I did not known Judy well at that time, and as her story unfolded, I was amazed that the life that spread such joy had held so much pain.

Because of the sensitive nature of some of the stories, I had told women that we could "change the names to protect the innocent," but Judy fired back, "Use my name! God has done so much for me; I want everyone to know it!" It is characteristic of Judy's honesty.

Judy's life did not begin idyllically. Her father was a heavy drinker and she and her siblings were often the objects of his verbal abuse. For Judy, the legacy of the chaotic home life was rebellion.

"We didn't go to church, so I had no other influence, other than my dad," said Judy. "And I didn't like him," she added, her dark eyes serious.

Judy found refuge in teenage romance and turned to sex when she was 15 or 16 years old. Even while acting out her rebellion at home, she was a good student. She couldn't wait to escape life with her family and go to college. She was tired of the non-stop drinking and arguments at home, but she was a girl without an anchor so she soon succumbed to a party life at college.

But the wild ways caught up with her when she discovered she was pregnant her senior year. Her parents were angry at first, but they went crazy when they learned the father of the baby was black. Judy was made to quit school and move home.

The days were filled with arguments and accusations and Judy was miserable after the freedom of college, but had no other choice.

In a chance encounter, she ran into her Physical Education teacher from high school who had become a Christian. She invited Judy to a get together at a Christian coffeehouse. Judy went since it was better than sitting home, but found herself in an environment she didn't understand. She was attracted to the joy and freedom she saw in the young adults at the meeting. She heard stories and testimonies of people's lives changed by meeting Jesus. With no church background, it was a new world. The stories were captivating and Judy gave her life to the Lord.

The change was immediate and though her father couldn't understand her turning to religion, he "sure liked the change."

At that time, Judy hated men, including her dad. She had held onto buried, deep anger and bitterness toward him and now it was being washed away with Jesus' love. Though he couldn't accept it for himself, Judy's dad easily recognized the change in his rebellious daughter. It was the testimony of a changed life.

The same night Judy got saved, she met a tall, good-looking guy named Rich Epp. He was already a Christian and she was attracted to his kindness and good looks. They soon became a couple and married with Judy still pregnant!

The only answer seemed to be to give the baby up for adoption so as soon as her little boy was born; he was taken from Judy and placed with a loving family.

The grief was immediate and overwhelming. Everyone told her she was doing the right thing, but it didn't feel right. Life went on around her as if nothing had happened, while Judy grieved alone. Everyone else had moved on, but she couldn't seem to. She was mired in anger and guilt. God had given her a new life and a wonderful husband, so why was she so unhappy?

When anger and guilt moved into the neighborhood, bitterness soon followed stealing Judy's joy. Judy knew the price God had paid for her life, so she struggled with the feelings of anger, but she didn't know what to do to change them. Anger was the foundational brick on the wall Judy built between herself and God. She buried the anger as best she could and got on with life.

But the feeling of loss and that a piece of her life was missing did not go away. And the anger wouldn't stay buried.

As the Epp family grew, Judy's home was full, but her heart still grieved over the little boy she'd given away. Judy loved Kacy, Kristi, Keni and Kody, but she wondered about the life of her first born being raised by a different mother.

Holidays were hardest as she grieved at the empty place where her oldest son would have been. Many nights she sat alone crying for the child that was not there to share Christmas with the family.

Looking back, Judy says she was a horrible wife and mom. She had no confidence in her ability to love her husband and her children. She maintained her distance from God while going through the motions of being a Christian wife and mother.

But when she would see those who had experienced deep sorrow in their own lives and risen above it, she longed to do the same.

Psalms 30:5 says "weeping may last for the night, but joy will come in the morning." Judy was intimately acquainted with weeping and sorrow as she struggled in the dark night of her soul, but she couldn't find a pathway to lead her out of the darkness and into the joy of the dawn.

She remained active at church, but never let anyone get too close. The other women only knew the "surface" Judy. She was filled with shame and apprehensive someone would discover the "real" Judy and learn about the woman she used to be. Judy was almost broken by the burden of pretending and life was not easy in the Epp house.

Thinking about Judy, I am reminded of the story of the elephant in the living room that no one talks about.

Everyone in the family walks around the elephant and pretends that it is perfectly all right for the elephant to be there even though it takes up lots of room, is messy and smells bad! They feed it and care for it among the couches and chairs, pretending everything is just fine.

In Judy's family, the children knew of Judy's deep sadness and that she'd given their brother up for adoption, but no one acknowledged the deep pain in the family over that decision. No one acknowledged the price that Judy had paid and what it had cost her. They just walked around the elephant, going to church or school or work, doing their best to live a good life.

When I asked, Judy wasn't sure why she was unable to get help from God during this time, but then admitted that she stayed away from the word of God and kept a wall up to keep others out so that no one would know "what I was."

All that changed when Judy's dad died from a massive heart attack. Judy felt compelled that her son should know of the family history of sudden death, so she wrote to the adoption agency and asked that the information be put in her son's file, along with a note that she'd like to meet him. Previously she'd tried to find him, but had given up. This time, when the adoption agency sent information back to her, enclosed was a flyer about an agency that reunites adopted children and their birthparents.

God's timing is perfect.

Several weeks later she found him, living an hour away from her, but he was unsure about meeting her. Judy was heartbroken, but a few days later his mom called Judy to say that he would be leaving for the Navy in a few days and was considering meeting her before he left. Judy was overjoyed. When he learned he'd be going to Japan soon, he finally agreed to meet her.

It was an emotional reunion for the 19 year old soldier and his mom, but the most significant thing the handsome young man said to her was, "I forgive you" for placing him for adoption. A huge burden lifted with his words and Judy was freed from the millstone of guilt she'd carried for almost 20 years.

But with the lessening of one burden came another. Judy's brother, who was so significant to Kacy's story, committed suicide. He had been an alcoholic with a life of many ups and downs, but even so, this was unexpected and devastating.

Judy voice was almost inaudible when she spoke of her brother's death. She grieves that her brother "threw his life away." They hadn't been close through the years, but there had been times she'd helped him dig out of the pit of depression, but this time it was too deep.

But God is faithful and Judy comforts herself by remembering the many times she talked to him about the Lord. There had been times she'd been accused of "at him, but instead she chooses to remember the day when he was twelve and she talked to him about Jesus, her Savior. That day, Judy prayed with him as he accepted the Lord and she believes she will see him in heaven. Judy also finds joy that Kacy's life was changed by the goodness of her brother's heart to reach out to his hurting niece when she was at the lowest point of her life. She and Kacy both question how he could have been so used by God as a messenger of His love, throwing Kacy a life line that he could not grab for himself.

But those two events—finding her son and his forgiveness and losing her brother caused Judy to stop and remember the freshness and joy of the Living Water served in that Christian coffeehouse so long ago. Water that she'd gladly drank deeply of until the anger and bitterness stole it away.

I'm reminded of Matthew 13 where Jesus tells the parable of the sower. He tells how good seeds were sown on the path, but birds came and ate the seeds. Other seeds fell on the rocky ground so there wasn't much soil to sustain them. Plants sprang up, but when the sun came out, the plants were scorched and withered away. Other seeds fell among the thorns so that the plants were choked by the weeds.

But some seed fell on the good ground and produced a good crop.

As Jesus explains the parable, he tells of the evil one coming and snatching what was sown in the heart. And how the seeds on rocky ground are those who receive the word with joy, but they have no roots, so when trouble comes, they stumble.

We are all like this story of the seeds, including Judy.

Because of the lies of Satan, though we accept Christ, we continue to believe a delusion.

"You're not good enough! Don't you remember what you've done! They don't know what you're really like! If they did, do you think they'd care about you?"

We continue to go through the motions, still attracted to the Gospel, but somehow convinced Jesus made a mistake when he saved us. We don't grow and we don't bear fruit. Like Adam and Eve, we begin to hide thinking God won't notice we're there and maybe let us stay with the "good" people.

Judy spent a lifetime feeling ashamed of who she was. Her relationship with her earthly father colored her relationship with her heavenly father. She saw others in church worshiping and praying, looked at their happy faces and thought she didn't belong. And wondered why she didn't feel the same. On the outside, she looked like everyone else, but deep inside, the still small voice she heard sounded suspiciously like her dad saying, "I know what you really are."

After losing her brother, Judy finally was exhausted with pretending. She was tired of holding it all together on the outside, doing her best to look joyful when her heart was breaking.

In surrender, she prayed, "God, it's yours." And she finally surrendered *everything*—the anger, the hurt, the pain, the bitterness and most importantly, the past.

Part of the healing process was counseling with a godly older woman who took her through the Scriptures teaching her what God says about "who she is" in Christ. For the first time, she could separate her dad's voice from God's voice and she realized that she wasn't all those things that her dad called her. Judy was not a slutty whore but a daughter of the King!

Judy realized something key for many of us. That she'd never understood the unconditional love of God because she had never experienced unconditional love from her own dad. Her father had gotten mixed up with God, the Father. The unrighteousness judgment of her earthly father had overshadowed the righteous judgment of the Father who loved her so much He sent Jesus to die for her.

When she was able to see God's truth and who He said she is and who He says He is, she could finally fully drink the Living Water for herself!

But it was hard. It meant giving up the lie that everything was just fine. It took surrender and exchanging the lie for the Truth.

Like so many of us, when Judy finally surrendered it was because she was too tired to do anything else.

The weary woman at the well was ready to surrender, too. Like the cartoon of the frazzled, weary woman standing in her messy kitchen waving a white dish towel while several toddlers play with broken dishes at her feet, saying, "I'd surrender, if I just knew who to surrender to," she was ready.

Both Judy and the woman figured out who to surrender to.

He was waiting for them.

Beloved, are you ready to surrender it all?

The woman who ran down the path to Sychar was not the same woman who had trudged up the path minutes before.

STORIES FROM THE WELL 89

The woman who got up from her knees after praying, "God it's yours!" was not the same woman who knelt on the carpet moments before.

Surrender does that for a person!

Life changes because God can get to work! When we stop trying to work *for* God and let *Him work on us and in us and through us,* it changes everything!

The woman ran down the path and back to those who'd hurt her to tell them the good news! She put aside her own agenda to take up Christ's agenda.

There were probably still those who rejected her, but it no longer mattered!

The King of Kings had accepted her!

For the first time, like Judy, she knew she wasn't what they said she was!

For the first time, like Judy, she knew *who* she was and she knew *whose* she was! And that made all the difference.

It probably was not a primrose path. Like the parable of the sower, the enemy was there with different faces and names to bring doubt again.

Can you imagine the scene when she went home and said, "I can't live with you any more until you marry me!" or "I am worth getting married to, and I'd like us to be married, but I need to tell you, it's going to be different!" Or even, "I'm sorry. I've been with you because I had no place else to go, but I don't like how you treat me— like I'm dirt. I'm not dirt. So I have to leave you and find another place to live."

Can you imagine the scene over the next days and weeks as the woman is effervescent with joy and laughter on the way to the well? Her face even looks different. Younger. Beautiful. Softer now as the morning light illuminates her olive skin. A spring in her step and life in her eyes.

I can imagine a few catty remarks. Those who've walked on you don't particularly like it when their doormat gets up and walks beside them!

But the woman just smiles hearing the voice that only she can hear. It is the voice of the King, singing to her, "You are my beloved!" It makes all the difference when you walk to the well knowing the one who loves you has given you everything you need and you'll never worry about water again!

Judy is the ebullient, joy-filled woman I know today because she accepted her identity from Christ, not from the past. And as she drank of the Living Water, her life changed. Now she runs down the path to everyone she knows to tell them the good news! There truly is New Life in Christ!

"Here! You look thirsty! Do you need a drink? Let me tell you about the water I have! There is more than enough and it is for you!"

Beloved, are you drinking the water of the King? If not, don't waste another moment! Drink up!

Or Beloved, if you've been to the well, who have you taken with you and offered a drink today?

Dear Lord,

Thank you that You love me no matter where I've been or what I've done. Lord, let me hear Your voice singing over me! Fill me to overflowing with Your living water that I might never thirst again. And give me water that I might take it to a thirsty world in Your name.

Lord, help me to see those who have lost their joy and give them a drink. Lord, show me those who say they know You, but they listen to lies from the enemy about who they are in You. Lord, let me pour buckets of Living Water over them!

Thank you, Lord that You are an extravagant God and You love me with an extravagant Love. Give me divine appointments to share that love with others.

In Jesus' name,
Amen.

"I will give to the thirsty from the spring of living water as a gift." Revelations 21:6

Thirteen

STREAMS OF LIVING WATER

Neva Miller went to heaven last week. And if I were a betting person, I'd bet that the angels who had been singing to her the last three years of her 89 year life rejoiced as she entered the gates.

Neva called the music her "heart music" because she heard it with her heart, not her ears, but I am sure in heaven she heard it with every part of her—ears, heart and whole being—as she was welcomed home.

The Bible says those who know the Lord are saints. (Phil 4:21, for one example).

When someone says that in relation to me, I know there are some that would question my sainthood, especially those that live with me everyday! But Neva was one of those sweet women that it takes no stretch of the imagination to see her as a saint.

She came from a family of hard working Kansas farmers. Godly, salt of the earth people whose leisure time was spent together discussing things of importance. Farm life, church, family, the weather and crops, and of course, the things of God.

A favorite pastime was singing hymns in harmony with her sisters sitting on the wide front porch, their voices wafting on the warm evening breezes of Kansas summers.

Neva learned about God, the Father, by watching her father, Thaddeus, who was a gentle, quiet and godly man as he responded patiently to the whims of Kansas weather that could ruin the crops he'd worked so hard to plant in the rich fertile soil.

Some of us pray as a last resort, but Neva learned that prayer was the answer for the headaches and heartaches of life.

Her son, Pastor Scott Miller, says that raising eight children automatically made her an intercessor! Neva prayed for her children, yes, but her whole life was one of praying for those she loved and that included family, friends and strangers as she was led.

Even in the end of her life, as her body failed her, her mind was occupied with prayer.

At the end of her years, Neva was blind, but could see lights around her feet. She believed that Jesus was showing her just where to walk. With failing eyesight, she never lost sight of her Savior and clearly saw the things of God.

It was with unwavering faith that she lived and died. She raised her eight children at a time with few of the modern conveniences we take for granted.

Sacrificially, she devoted her time to getting up before the family rose to put the coffee pot on and make a good breakfast for everyone. Son Scott remembers a time he had to get up at 4:30 in the morning to go fishing and the thought occurred to him that that was too early even for his mom, but she was up when he tiptoed into the kitchen before 4:30 with coffee and his breakfast waiting. He says it was then that he knew how much she loved him.

She not only taught and served as an example of faith and sacrificial love to her children, but to many others as well. She was a Sunday school teacher for 67 years—from the time she was 14 years of age until her eyesight failed in 1998. She was awarded the Kansas Sunday School Teacher of the Year award in 1996.

She was a woman that Paul taught we should emulate in the book of Titus—a mature woman who mentors younger women. Neva mentored through a weekly breakfast group. The lasting legacy of Neva Miller is that even after she could no longer take part in the group, the group continued and still meets today. Neva put her heart and time into the things that are eternal.

When one of the Pharisee's came to Jesus asking Him what the greatest commandment was, Jesus replied that it was to love God with all your heart, soul, mind and strength and to love your neighbor as yourself. (Matt. 22:35-40)

Neva understood the greatest commandment because her whole life was consumed with loving God and loving others. She lived the greatest commandment for 89 years, but she also understood what Christ meant when he taught his disciples that love means service. It was one of the last things that he taught them when he washed their feet at the Last Supper.

In Luke 22:27b Christ said, "But I am among you as one who serves." There is no doubt that Neva understood those words of Christ, because one of her greatest joys was her service to others. It was a beacon of light guiding others to the light of Christ

Serving is not easy. We are selfish creatures by nature. As Paul said, (my paraphrase) "The things I don't want to do, I do and those I want to do I don't do! Oh wretched man am I!" (Roman 7:14-24)

So many times in my life, I have known the right thing to do or the loving thing to do or the serving thing to do, but my flesh wants what it wants!

Perhaps Neva struggled with this as well, but if she did, it was a private struggle. What the world saw was a woman who loved God and who loved people.

How did she do it?

I believe it was because she had found the streams of living water and lived her life as a tree planted by His stream of living water.

"How happy is the man who does not follow the advice of the wicked, or take the path of sinners, or join the group of mockers! Instead, his delight is in the Lord's instruction, and he meditates on it day and night. *He is like a tree planted beside streams of water that bears its fruit in season and whose leaf does not wither. Whatever he does prospers.*" Psalm 1:1-3

In the last weeks of Neva's life, her physical body failed and she could not process any food or water. It was necessary to have a tube placed in her nose to drain out everything from her stomach, even water. Her son, Scott, and daughter-in-law, Wanda, would give her sips of water so that she could wet her mouth, but the tube would immediately pump the precious liquid back out of her body again.

She was so thirsty in those weeks.

The water soothed her parched mouth and tongue, but there was no way to soothe the thirst of her body.

But because Neva had another supply, she rejoiced at each drink of water she was given and prayed for those who might be thirsty.

She would take a sip of cool, life giving water and rejoice at the wonderful taste of it. And then she would say, "I've been praying to Jesus that He wouldn't let any children or anybody go to bed without a drink of water!"

Neva had discovered the secret of life! When Jesus had offered her the Living Water, she drank deeply and never stopped.

In John 7:37b-38, Jesus stands up and cries out, "If anyone is thirsty, he should come to me and drink! The one who believes in Me, as the Scripture has said, will have streams of living water flow from deep within him."

Neva could pray for others to have their thirst quenched even as she was desperately thirsty because she believed in Him and the Living Water flowed deeply within her!

The water the woman came for that day was from the ancient well that the patriarch, Jacob, had dug. He had satisfied his thirst at that well as had his sons and his livestock.

That water had a great pedigree!

She filled the jar with as much as it would hold. And then a stranger asked her for a drink.

Jesus knew her jar was full, but the water was lacking for what the woman needed. And soon the water would be used, the jar emptied and she would trudge up that rocky path one more time. You cannot give what you do not have.

Do you think she begrudged the man who wanted to take the water she worked so hard to get?

Beloved, there will always be those who need a drink.

Where does your water come from?

Dr. Greg Baer, in his "Real Love"[7] video series, describes what happens when our love banks are empty. I'll paraphrase his illustration:

If you were holding two dollars in your hand and someone ran up and stole your last two dollars, how would you feel? You needed those two dollars to buy you something to eat or a gallon of gas for your car and it was all you had. It would make you angry!

But what if you were holding two dollars and someone ran up and grabbed the two dollars out of your hand. But you knew you had two million dollars in the bank! You would probably just laugh. You wouldn't even be annoyed that someone had taken two dollars from you because you knew you had plenty more.

Changes everything, doesn't it?

That, Beloved, is the difference between going to the well yourself versus accepting his offer to jump into the River of Life where the love of God and the Living Water flows!

When you have plenty of water, you have plenty to offer to others. You can live the life of love and service that characterized Neva Miller's life. You can open your heart and arms wide and let his love flow through you.

So let's turn the spigot on and become a conduit of His love!

When you open your heart to His love and sacrifice, when you speak His truth, believe His truth and live His truth in your life, the freeing, filling, cleansing, thirst relieving Living Water flows in and you'll never thirst again!

But what flows in must flow out!

Being filled with His love allows you to love Him with all of your heart, soul, mind and strength. Loving Him that way allows you to love and serve others as you do yourself. And as you are Christ's hands and feet and heart in a lost and dying world, you become like Christ and the Living Water flows out of you! Better yet, it gushes out of you!

But no matter. It never runs dry.

You have come to the River of Living Water, to the deep places of God where He dwells!

Drink deeply! Fill yourself! You will never be the same!

In Rev. 21:6 it says, "I will give to the thirsty from the spring of living water as a gift."

I can only imagine Neva dancing through the gates of heaven as she makes her way to the river of Living Water that sparkles like crystal and flows from the throne of God and of the Lamb down the middle of the broad street of the city. On both sides of the river grow the trees of life.

Father God smiles as Jesus says, "Yes, Father, it's Neva, I know her well!"

It is a royal welcome for this servant of the Most High God! She is welcomed into the Kingdom by the King himself, given a royal gift taken from the overflowing, vibrant, spring of Living Water.

Neva's voice is strong and melodious as she hums a familiar song with the angelic chorus. Her once dim eyes are bright with health and happiness as they take in all of His Kingdom, but mostly, she cannot take her eyes off the King.

He offers her a goblet of the finest crystal filled to overflowing with sparkling water. She takes the tiniest sip of the gift he offers, savoring the cool, moist, water in her mouth. It is familiar and at the same time like nothing she has ever tasted, but she knows one thing—her thirst is over! She lifts the goblet to her lips, drinking deeply of the fragrant, refreshing water again and again.

"Oh, it tastes so good, Lord. It tastes so good!"

My Prayer for You

Beloved,

Thank you for coming along with me on this journey to the well. I pray you think of the lonely woman who walked to the well that day a little differently. And I pray you will remember my story and the stories of the others who have been to the well before you and found Jesus waiting there. But more than anything else, I pray that you met Jesus on this journey in a new and fresh way and you have been filled as only He can satisfy!

God bless you. You are in my prayers. I leave you with this...

From "The Message"[8] by Eugene Peterson

Ephesians 3-6 How blessed is God! And what a blessing he is! He's the Father of our Master, Jesus Christ, and takes us to the high places of blessing in him. Long before he laid down earth's foundations, he had us in mind, had settled on us as the focus of his love, to be made whole and holy by his love. Long, long ago he decided to adopt us into his family through Jesus Christ. (What pleasure he took in planning this!) He wanted us to enter into the celebration of his lavish gift-giving by the hand of his beloved Son.

7-10 Because of the sacrifice of the Messiah, his blood poured out on the altar of the Cross, we're a free people—free of penalties and punishments chalked up by all our misdeeds. And not just barely free, either. Abundantly free! He thought of everything, provided for everything we could possibly need, letting us in on the plans he took such delight in making. He set it all out before us in Christ, a long-range plan in which everything would be brought together and summed up in him, everything in deepest heaven, everything on planet earth.

11-12 It's in Christ that we find out who we are and what we are living for. Long before we first heard of Christ and got our hopes up, he had his eye on us, had designs on us for glorious living, part of the overall purpose he is working out in everything and everyone.

13-14 It's in Christ that you, once you heard the truth and believed it (this Message of your salvation), found yourselves home free—signed, sealed, and delivered by the Holy Spirit. This signet from God is the first installment on what's coming, a reminder that we'll get everything God has planned for us, a praising and glorious life.

15-19 That's why, when I heard of the solid trust you have in the Master Jesus and your outpouring of love to all the followers of Jesus, I couldn't stop thanking God for you—every time I prayed, I'd think of you and give thanks. But I do more than thank. I ask—ask the God of our Master, Jesus Christ, the God of glory—to make you intelligent and discerning in knowing him personally, your eyes focused and clear, so that you can see exactly what it is he is calling you to do, grasp the immensity of this glorious way of life he has for his followers, oh, the utter extravagance of his work in us who trust him—endless energy, boundless strength!

20-23 All this energy issues from Christ: God raised him from death and set him on a throne in deep heaven, in charge of running the universe, everything from galaxies to governments, no name and no power exempt from his rule. And not just for the time being, but forever. He is in charge of it all, has the final word on everything. At the center of all this, Christ rules the church. The church, you see, is not peripheral to the world; the world is peripheral to the church. The church is Christ's body, in which he speaks and acts, by which he fills everything with his presence.

Amen and Amen!
~Kim Zweygardt
Jan. 1, 2007

Endnotes

1. "I'm A Woman" written by Jerry Leiber & Mike Stoller, recorded by Maria Muldaur
2. Enjoli Fragrance commercial circa 1970's
3. "Washed in the Blood", Elisha A. Hoffman, Cleveland, Ohio, Barker & Smellie, 1878
4. "Nothing But the Blood", Robert Lowery, New York, Bigelow & Main, 1876
5. Wikipedia.org/wiki/Imago_Dei
6. Nancy Leigh DeMoss, Radio Program host, Revive Our Hearts, Dec. 2006
7. Greg Baer, M.D., The Essentials of Real Love, Blue Ridge Press
8. The Message New Testament, Copyright 1993 by Eugene Peterson, NavPress, Colorado Springs, CO